S0-BYO-589

IT WAS NOT UNTIL FEBRUARY 14 THAT THE GOVERNMENT DECLARED A STATE OF EMERGENCY . . .

Syndic leaders had occupied and fortified George Washington High School, with the enthusiastic cooperation of students, faculty, and neighborhood . . .

At 5:15 A.M. the First Battalion of the 27th Armored Division took up positions . . .

By 5:26 Syndic contract pilots were airborn from their secret fields, but this time the smugglers' cargo was air-to-ground missiles that moments later were whipping into the tanks of the 27th.

The trial by fire had begun.

REVISED AND WITH A FOREWORD AND AFTERWORD BY

FREDERIK POHL

a novel that in its original edition was called
"FAR MORE POWERFUL THAN 1984"—The New York <u>Daily News</u>
and
"MARKEDLY SUPERIOR TO ALL THE REST"—<u>Kirkus</u>

by an author
**"AS GOOD AT GIVING US SURPRISING
INSIGHTS THAT ILLUMINATE THE WORLD WE LIVE IN
AS ANY WRITER WHO HAS EVER LIVED"**
—Frederik Pohl

Now, <u>Not This August</u> reads like tomorrow,
complete with laser ABMs, cruise missiles, stealth penetration, and more.
But its message remains timeless.

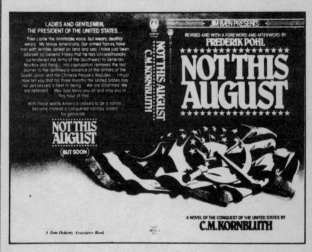

"NOT THIS AUGUST IS WITTY, POWERFUL AND ILLUMINATING."
—Frederik Pohl

TOR BOOKS
WE'RE PART OF THE FUTURE

THE SYNDIC

BY
C.M. KORNBLUTH

TOR

A TOM DOHERTY ASSOCIATES BOOK

THE SYNDIC

This is a work of fiction. All the characters and events portrayed in this book are fictional, and any resemblance to real people or incidents is purely coincidental.

Copyright © 1953 by C. M. Kornbluth

All rights reserved, including the right to reproduce this book, or portions thereof in any form.

Material original to this edition copyright ©1982 by TOR Books.

A TOR Book

First TOR printing, September, 1982

ISBN: 523-48543-3

Cover art by Howard Chaykin

Printed in the United States of America

Distributed by:

Pinnacle Books, Inc.
1430 Broadway
New York, New York 10018

The Syndic

by C. M. Kornbluth

With an Introduction and Afterword by Frederik Pohl, and a Personal Memoir by H. L. Gold

Frederik Pohl

Introduction to THE SYNDIC, by
C. M. Kornbluth

The Syndic takes place just after the Second
American Revolution—a time, that is, not too
far from now, when the freedom-loving citizens of the United States have once more
risen up to throw off the tyrants' yoke. Who
are the tyrants? Why, they're the folks that
the First American Revolution put in power.
At least they're their latter-day descendants,
namely the ones who inhabit the Capital and
the White House—and all those other bas-
tions of power like the Pentagon, the J. Edgar
Hoover Building that houses the F.B.I., the
Supreme Court and, most of all, the Internal
Revenue Service. And who are the freedom
fighters? Why, they're the Mafia. Who else?
This is the kind of stand-everything-on-its
head notion that Cyril Kornbluth loved to
play with, and, of course, he does it very well.

Rereading *The Syndic* for what must easily be the eighth or tenth time, I found it still startled laughter out of me. And it is full of those Kornbluth people who don't seem to show up in anybody else's novels. There must be fifteen or twenty characters in *The Syndic*, drunks and desperados, gangsters and heroes, every one of whom comes to life for you in three fully rounded dimensions in just a couple of lines. James Blish was awed by Cyril's ability to make human beings of all varieties seem solid and real, in very little space; I share his awe.

There are people who find a great deal more in *The Syndic* than that, though. One Libertarian I know calls it a political tract of the highest order—the actual words he used were "sacred writing" for the Libertarian cause. Probably that is why the *Laissez Faire Review*'s literary critic, J. Neil Schulman, called *The Syndic* "a vastly entertaining and insightful projection of a successful libertarian society . . . . A science fiction novel even Dr. Rothbard might like"—and why, when a Libertarian group in science fiction proposed to give annual awards for the best novels in that area, their first thought was to call the awards "Cyrils".

Cyril Kornbluth was born in 1923 and died in 1958, the delayed result of injuries to his heart received as a U.S. Army machine-gunner in the Battle of the Bulge. He and I were close friends for most of his life—as well as collaborators on novels like *The Space*

Merchants and others, some of them not
science fiction. I know that he went through a
brief teen-age interest in Marxism (as I did),
and that he considered Franklin D. Roosevelt
the greatest possible president for his times
(as I also did); but I really do not know any
more than that about what his political opin-
ions were. For the last decade of his life or so,
I suspect he had none, except a sort of general
dislike and contempt for nearly all political
leaders of the time. From what (little) I know
about Libertarians, that's not far from their
central philosophy . . . but also not all that far
from a lot of Republicans, Democrats and
down-the-middle non-partisans, too. So much
the worse for all of us.

Brian Stableford, writing in Peter Nich-
oll's *The Science Fiction Encyclopedia*, pays
high tribute to Cyril Kornbluth's writing
(particularly to his short stories), with
phrases like "graceful writing", "elegant con-
struction" and "deeply ingrained with bitter
irony", and considers *The Syndic* the best of
his solo novels. I respect Stableford's judgment, but am not able to select one of Cyril's
novels as "best"—they are all quite different,
and all very good in his very individual way.
But I think it's fair to say that *The Syndic* is
most truly Cyril's own voice speaking, in
tones no other writer has quite succeeded in
capturing.

I suppose it's possible that long friendship
with Cyril makes those tones, or at least a few
of the grace-notes, more recognizable to me.
Let me share one of the grace notes. Old-time

Futurians played games with each other, and one of them was to give each other little digs in their fiction. In *Gunner Cade* (one of the two science-fiction novels Cyril wrote in collaboration with Judith Merril), there is a sniveling, mean-spirited petty punk who plays an important, if whiney part. Around that time Judy Merril's four-year-old daughter was still having trouble with complicated names; the closest to mine she could come was "Threadwick"—and that's the name of the sniveling punk. (The ways in which I then got back at Cyril and Judy any interested scholar is welcome to seek out for himself.) There's one of those in *The Syndic*. One of Cyril's and my close friends in the middle 1950s, when *The Syndic* was written, was Fletcher Pratt, not only a worthy science-fiction writer but also a historian, perhaps best known for his marvelous one-volume story of the Civil War, *Ordeal by Fire*. So when Cyril wanted to cite a madeup historian in this novel, he named him, of course, B. Arrowsmith Hynde.

There's one other grace note in the novel worth mentioning, although it was surely not intended at the time. The inept political boss of Middle America in *The Syndic* happens to have a name closely resembling that of another, more recent political leader of some fame. That one, however, must surely be labeled a simple coincidence . . . I think.

— Frederik Pohl

"It was not until February 14 that the Government declared a state of unlimited emergency. The precipitating incident was the aerial bombardment and destruction of B Company, 27th Armored Regiment, on Fort George Hill in New York City. Local Syndic leaders had occupied and fortified George Washington High School, with the enthusiastic cooperation of students, faculty, and neighborhood. Chief among them was Thomas 'Numbers' of Cleveland, displaying the same coolness and organizational genius which had brought him to preeminence in the metropolitan policy-wheel organization by his thirty-fifth year.

"At 5:15 A.M. the 1st Battalion of the 27th Armored took up positions in the area' as follows: A Company at 190th Street and St. Nicholas Avenue, with the mission of pre-

venting reinforcement of the school from the
IRT subway station there; Companies B, C,
and D hull down from the school on the slope
of Fort George Hill poised for an attack. At
5:25 the sixteen Main Battle Tanks of B Company revved up and moved on the school, C
and D companies remaining in reserve. The
plan was for the tanks of B Company to sur-
round the school on three sides—the fourth is
a precipice—and open fire if a telephone
parley with Cleveland did not result in an un-
conditional surrender.

"Cleveland's observation post was in the
tower room of the school. Seeing the radio
mast of the lead tank top the rise of the hill, he
snapped out a telephone order to contract
pilots waiting for the word at a Syndic field
floating outside the seven-mile limit. The
pilots, trained to split-second precision in
their years of public service, were airborne by
5:26, but this time their cargo was not liquor,
cigarettes, or luggage. In three minutes, they
were whipping rocket bombs into the tanks of
Company B; Cleveland's runners charged the
company command post; the trial by fire had
begun.

"Before it ended North America was to see
deeds as gallant and strategy as inspired as
any in the history of war: Cleveland's historic
announcement—'It's a great day for the race!'
—his death at the head of his runners in a
charge on the Fort Totten garrison, the firm
hand of Amadeo Falcaro taking up the scat-
tered reins of leadership, parley, peace, betrayal, and execution of hostages, the Treaty

of Las Vegas and a united Mob-Syndic front against Government, O'Toole's betrayal of the Continental Press wire-room and the bloody battle to recapture that crucial nerve center, the decisive March on Baltimore . . . ."

> B. Arrowsmith Hynde,
> *The Syndic—A Short History*

When in your courses make no spells
    For you have no power;
You shall not drink from duggen wells
    Or give your hand in dower.

Snares may you set of bark and vine
    Taking coney and deer;
You shall not hunt with the deathly wine
    Tipped on the broadblade spear.

She who is in you hates the steel;
    It was her downfall.
Hunt down the smithymen and deal
    Death to them all.

Until thirteen moons times thirteen
    You shall not know a man.
She who is in you, she the queen,
    Then lifts the ban.

> From *Instruction for Witches,*
> c. 2150 A.D.

"No accurate history of the future has ever been written—a fact which I think disposes of history's claim to rank as a science. Astronomers quail at the three-body problem and throw up their hands in surrender before the four-body problem. Any given moment in history is a problem of at least four billion bodies. Attempts at orderly abstraction of manipulable symbols from the realities of history seem to me doomed from the start. I can juggle mean rainfalls, car-loading curves, birthrates and patent applications, but I cannot for the life of me fit the recurring facial carbuncles of Karl Marx into my manipulations—not even, though we know, well after the fact, that agonizing staphylococcus aureus infections behind that famous beard helped shape twentieth century totalitarianism. In pathology alone the list could be prolonged indefinitely: Julius Caesar's epilepsy, Napoleon's gastritis, Wilson's paralysis, Grant's alcoholism, Wilhelm II's withered arm, Catherine's nymphomania, George III's paresis, Edison's deafness, Euler's blindness, Burke's stammer, and so on. Is there anybody silly enough to maintain that the world today would be what it is if Marx, Caesar, Napoleon, Wilson, Grant, Wilhelm, Catherine, George, Edison, Euler and Burke—to take only these eleven—had been anything but what they were? Yet that is the assumption behind theories of history which exclude the carbuncles of Marx from their referents—that is to say, every theory of history with which I am familiar.

"Am I, then, saying that history, past and future, is unknowable; that we must blunder ahead in the dark without planning because no plan can possibly be accurate in prediction and useful in application? I am not. I am expressing my distaste for holders of extreme positions, for possessors of eternal truths, for keepers of the flame. Keepers of the flame have no trouble with the questions of ends and means which plague the rest of us. They are quite certain that their ends are good and that therefore choice of means is a trivial matter. The rest of us, far from certain that we have a general solution of the four-billion-body problem that is history, are much more likely to ponder on our means . . . ."

F. W. Taylor
Organization, Symbolism and Morale

ONE

Charles Orsino was learning the business from the ground up—even though "up" would never be very high. He had in his veins only a drop or two of Falcaro blood: enough so that room had to be made for him; not enough for it to be a great deal of room. Counting heavily on the good will of F. W. Taylor, who had taken a fancy to him when he lost his parents in the Brookhaven Reactor explosion, he might rise to a rather responsible position in Alky, Horsewire, Callgirl Recruitment and Retirement, or whatever line he showed an aptitude for. But at twenty-two one spring day, he was merely serving a tour of duty as bagman attached to the 101st New York Police Precinct. A junior member of the Syndic customarily handled that job; you couldn't trust the cops not to squeeze their customers and pocket the difference.

He walked absently through the not unpleasant routine of the shakedown. His mind was on his early-morning practice session of polo, in which he had almost disgraced himself.

"Good afternoon, Mr. Orsino; a pleasure to see you again. Would you like a cold glass of beer while I get the loot?"

"No, but thanks very much, Mr. Lefko—I'm in training, you know. Wish I could take you up on it. Seven phones, isn't it, at ten carlos a phone?"

"That's right, Mr. Orsino, and I'll be with you as soon as I lay off the seventh at Hialeah; all the ladies went for a plater named Hearthmouse because they thought the name was cute and left me with a dutch book. I won't be a minute."

Lefko scuttled to a phone and dickered with another bookie somewhere while Charles absently studied the crowd of chattering, laughing horseplayers. ("Mister Orsino, did you come out to make a monkey of yourself and waste my time? Confound it, sir, you have just fifty round to a chukker and you must make them count!" He grinned unhappily. Old Gilby, the pro, could be abrasive when a bonehead play disfigured the game he loved. Charles had been sure Benny Grashkin's jeep would conk out in a minute—it had been sputtering badly enough—and that he would have had a dirt-cheap scoring shot while Benny changed mounts. But Gilby blew the whistle and wasn't interested in your finespun logic. "Confound it, sir, when will you young rufflers learn that you must crawl before you walk? Now let me see a team rush for the goal —and I mean *team*, Mr. Orsino!")

"*Here* we are, Mr. Orsino, and just in time. There goes the seventh."

Charles shook hands and left amid screams of "Hearthmouse! Hearthmouse!" from the lady bettors watching the screen.

*   *   *

High up in the Syndic Building, F. W. Taylor—Uncle Frank to Charles—was giving a terrific tongue-lashing to a big, stooped old man. Thornberry, president of the Chase National Bank, had pulled a butch and F. W. Taylor was blazing mad about it.

He snarled: "One more like this, Thornberry, and you are out on your padded can. When a respectable member of the Syndic chooses to come to you for a line of credit, you will in the future give it without any tomfool quibbling about security. You bankers seem to think this is the Middle Ages and that your bits of paper still have their old black magic.

"Disabuse yourself of the notion. Nobody except you believes in it. The Inexorable Laws of Economics are as dead as Dagon and Ishtar, and for the same reason. No more worshipers. You bankers can't shove anybody around any more. You're just a convenience, like the non-playing banker in a card game.

"What's real now is the Syndic. What's real about the Syndic is its own morale and the public's faith in it. Is that *clear*?"

Thornberry brokenly mumbled something about supply and demand.

Taylor sneered. "Supply and demand. Urim and Thummim. Show me a supply, Thornberry, show me a—oh, hell. I haven't time to waste re-educating you. Remember what I told you and don't argue. Unlimited credit to Syndic members. If they overdo it, *we'll* rectify the situation. Now, get out." And Thornberry did, with senile tears in his eyes.

At Mother Maginnis' Ould Sod Pub, Mother Maginnis pulled a long face when Charles Orsino came in. "It's always a pleasure to see you, Mr. Orsino, but I'm afraid this week it'll be no pleasure for you to see me."

She was always roundabout. "Why, what do you mean, Mrs. M.? I'm always happy to say hello to a customer."

"It's the business, Mr. Orsino. It's the business. You'll pardon me if I say that I can't see how to spare twenty-five carlos from the till, not if my life depended on it. I can go to fifteen, but so help me—"

Charles looked grave—graver than he felt. It happened every day. "You realize, Mrs. Maginnis, that you're letting the Syndic down. What would the people in Syndic Territory do for protection if everybody took your attitude?"

She looked sly. "I was thinking, Mr. Orsino, that a young man like you must have a way with the girls—" By a mighty unsubtle maneuver, Mrs. Maginnis' daughter emerged from the back room at that point and began demurely mopping the bar. "And," she continued, "sure, any young lady would consider it an honor to spend the evening with a young gentleman from the Syndic—"

"Perhaps," Charles said, rapidly thinking it over. He would infinitely rather spend the evening with a girl than at a Shakespeare revival as he had planned, but there were drawbacks. In the first place, it would be bribery. In the second place, he might fall for the girl and wake up with Mrs. Maginnis for his mother-in-law—a fate too nauseating to contemplate for more than a moment. In the third place, he had already bought the tickets for himself and bodyguard.

"About the shakedown," he said decisively. "Call it fifteen this week. If you're still doing badly next week, I'll have to ask for a look at your books—to see whether a regular reduction is in order."

She got the hint, and colored. Putting down fifteen carlos, she said: "Sure, that won't be necessary. I'm expecting business to take a turn for the better."

"Good, then." To show there were no hard feelings, he stayed for a moment to ask: "How are your husbands?"

"So-so. Alfie's on the road this week and Dinnie's got the rheumatism again but he can tend bar late, when it's slow."

"Tell him to drop around to the Medical Center and mention my name, Mrs. Maginnis. Maybe they can do something for him."

She glowed with thanks and he left.

It was pleasant to be able to do things for

nice people; it was pleasant to stroll along the sunny street acknowledging tipped hats and friendly words. (That team rush for the goal had been a sorry mess, but not his fault— quite. Vladek had loosed a premature burst from his fifty caliber at the ball, and sent it hurling off to the right; they had braked and backed with much grinding of gears to form V again behind it, when Gilby blew the whistle again.)

A nervous youngster in the National Press Service New York drop was facing his first crisis on the job. Trouble lights had flashed simultaneously on the Kansas City-New York, Hialeah-New York and Boston-New York trunks. He stood, paralyzed.

His supervisor took it in in a flash and banged open the circuit to Service. To the genial face that appeared on the screen, he snapped: "Trace Hialeah, Boston, and Kansas City—in that order, Micky."

Micky said: "Okay, pal," and vanished.

The supervisor turned to the youngster. "Didn't know what to do?" he asked genially. "Don't let it worry you. Next time you'll know. You noticed the order of priority?"

"Yes," the boy gulped.

"It wasn't an accident that I gave it to him that way. First, Hialeah because it was the most important. We get the bulk of our revenue from serving the horse-rooms—in fact, I understand we started as a horsewire exclusively. Naturally the horse-room customers pay for it in the long run, but they pay without pain. Nobody's forcing them to improve the breed, right?

"Second, Boston-New York trunk. That's common carrier while the Fair Grounds isn't running up there. We don't make any profit on common-carrier service, the rates are too low, but we owe it to the public that supports us.

"Third, Kansas City-New York. That's common carrier too, but with one terminal in Mob Territory. No reason why we should knock ourselves out for Regan and his boys, but after the other two are traced and closed, we'll get around to them. Think you got it straight now?"

"Yes," the youngster said.

"Good. Just take it easy."

The supervisor moved away to do a job of billing that didn't need immediate doing; he wanted to avoid the very appearance of nagging the boy. He wondered too, if he'd really put it over, and decided he hadn't. How could he, after all? It took years on the wires to get the feel. Slowly your motivation changed. You started by wanting to make a place for yourself and earn some dough. After years you realized, not with a blinding flash, but gradually, that you were working for quite another reason. Nice gang here that treats you right. Don't let the Syndic down. The customers pay for their fun and by God, you see that they get it or bust a gut trying.

On his way to the 101st Precinct station house, the ears of Charles Orsino burned as

he thought of the withering lecture that had
followed the blast on Gilby's whistle. "*Mister*
Orsino, is it or is it not your responsibility as
team captain to demand that a dangerous ball
be taken out of play? And did or did not that
last burst from Mr. Vladek beat the ball out of
round, thus giving rise to a distinct possibility
of dangerous ricochets?" The old man was
right of course, but it had been a pocked and
battered practice ball to start with; in practice sessions, you couldn't afford to be fussy
—not with regulation 18-inch armor steel
balls selling for thirty carlos each at the pro
shop.

He walked between the two green lamps of
the precinct station and dumped his bag on
the sergeant's desk. Immediately the sergeant
started a tale of woe: "Mr. Orsino, I don't like
to bother you with the men's personal
troubles, but I wonder if you could come
through with a hundred-carlo present for a
very deserving young fellow here. It's Patrol-
man Gibney, seven years in the old 101st and
not a black mark against him. One citation for
shooting it out with a burglar and another for
nabbing a past-post crook at Lefko's horse-
room. Gibney's been married for five years
and has two of the cutest kids you ever saw,
and you know that takes money. Now he
wants to get married again, he's crazy in love
with the girl and his first wife don't mind, she
says she can use a helping hand around the
house, and he wants to do the thing right with
a big wedding."

"If he can do it on a hundred, he's welcome

to it," Charles said, grinning. "Give him my best wishes." He divided the pile of bills into two orderly stacks, transferred a hundred carlos to one and pocketed the other.

He dropped it off at the Syndic Building, had an uninteresting dinner in one of its cafeterias and went to his furnished room downtown. He read a chapter in F. W. Taylor's—Uncle Frank's—latest book, *Organization, Symbolism and Morale*, couldn't understand a word he read, bathed and got out his evening clothes.

TWO

A thin and attractive girl entered a preposterously furnished room in the Syndic Building, arguing bitterly with a white-bearded, hawk-nosed old man.

"My dear ancestor," she began, with exaggerated patience.

"God damn it, Lee, don't call me an ancestor! Makes me feel as if I was dead already."

"You might as well be for all the sense you're talking."

"All right, Lee." He looked wounded and brave.

"Oh, I didn't mean to hurt your feelings, Edward—" She studied his face with suddenly narrowed eyes and her tone changed. "Listen, you old devil, you're not fooling me for a minute. I couldn't hurt your feelings with the blunt edge of an axe. You're not talking me into anything. It'd just be sending somebody to his death. Besides, they were both accidents." She turned and began to fiddle with a semicircular screen whose focus was a large and complicated chair. Three synchronized projectors bore on the screen.

The old man said very softly, "And what if they weren't? Tom McGurn and Bob were good men. None better. If the damn Government's knocking us off one by one, something ought to be done. And you seem to be the only person in a position to do it."

"Start a war," she said bitterly. "Sweep them from the seas. Wasn't Dick Reiner chanting that when I was in diapers?"

"Yes," the old man brooded. "And he's still chanting it now that you're in—whatever young ladies wear nowadays. Promise me something, Lee. If there's another try, will you help us out?"

"I am so sure there won't be," she said, "that I'll promise. And God help you, Edward, if you try to fake one. I've told you before and I tell you now that it's almost certain death."

Charles Orsino studied himself in a three-way mirror.

The evening suit was new; he wished the gunbelt were. The holster rode awkwardly on his hip; he hadn't got a new outfit since his eighteenth birthday and his chest had filled out to the last hole of the cross-strap's buckle since then. Well, it would have to wait; the evening would cost him enough as it was. Five bodyguards! He winced at the thought. But you had to be seen at these things and you had to do it right or it didn't count.

He fell into a brief reverie of meeting a beautiful, beautiful girl at the theater, a girl who would think he was interesting and handsome and a wonderful polo player, a girl who would happily turn out to be in the direct Falcaro line with all sorts of powerful relations to speak up for him . . . .

Someone said on his room annunciator: "The limousine is here, Mr. Orsino. I'm Halloran, your chief bodyguard."

"Very well, Halloran," he said casually, just as he'd practiced it in the bathroom that morning, and rode down.

The limousine was a beauty and the guards were faultlessly turned out. One was democratic with one's chief guard and a little less so with the others. As Halloran drove, Charles chatted with him about the play, which was *Julius Caesar* in modern dress. Halloran said he'd heard it was very good.

Their arrival in the lobby of the Costello created no sensation. Five bodyguards wasn't a lot of bodyguards, even though there seemed to be no other Syndic people there. So much for the beautiful Falcaro girl. Charles chatted with a television director he knew slightly. The director explained to him that the theater was sick, very sick, that Harry Tremaine—he played Brutus—made a magnificent stage picture but couldn't read lines.

By then Halloran was whispering in his ear that it was time to take their seats. Halloran was sweating like a pig and Charles didn't get around to asking him why. Charles took an

aisle seat, Halloran was across the aisle and
the others sat to his side, front and rear.

The curtain rose on "New York—A Street."

The first scene, a timekiller designed to let
fidgeters subside and coughers finish their
coughing, was a 3-D projection of Times
Square, with a stylized suggestion of a public
relations consultant's office "down in one" on
the apron.

When Caesar entered Orsino started, and
there was a gratified murmur around the
auditorium. He was made up as French
Letour, one of the Mobsters from the old days
—technically a hero, but one who had sailed
mighty close to the wind. This promised to be
interesting.

"Peace, ho! Caesar speaks."

And so to the apron where the soothsayer
—public relations consultant—delivered the
warning contemptuously ignored by Letour-
Caesar, and the spotlight shifted to Cassius
and Brutus for their long, foreboding dia-
logue. Brutus' back was to the audience when
it started; he gradually turned—

"What means this shouting? I do fear the
  people

Choose Caesar for their king!"

And you saw that Brutus was Falcaro—old
Amadeo Falcaro himself, with the beard and
hawk nose and eyebrows.

Well, let's see now. It must be some kind of
tortured analogy with the Treaty of Las Vegas
when Letour made a strong bid to unite Mob
and Syndic and Falcaro had fought against
anything but a short-term, strictly military

alliance. Charles felt kind of sore about Falcaro not getting the title role, but he had to admit that Tremaine played Falcaro as the gusty magnifico he had been. When Caesar re-entered, the contrast became clear; Caesar-Letour was a fidgety, fear-ridden man. The rest of the conspirators brought on through Act One turned out to be good fellows all, fresh and hearty; Charles guessed everything was all right and he wished he could grab a nap. But Cassius was saying:

"Him and his worth and our great need of him—"

All very loyal, Charles thought, smothering a yawn. A life for the Syndic and all that, but a highbrow version. Polite and dignified, like a pavane at Roseland. Sometimes—after, say, a near miss on the polo field—he would wonder how polite and dignified the great old days actually had been. Amadeo Falcaro's Third-Year Purge must have been an affair of blood and guts. Two thousand shot in three days, the history books said, adding hastily that the purged were unreconstructed, unreconstruct-able thugs whose usefulness was past, who couldn't realize that the job ahead was con-struction and organization.

And Halloran was touching Charles on the shoulder. "Intermission in a second, sir."

They marched up the aisle as the curtain fell to applause and the rest of the audience began to rise. Then the impossible happened.

Halloran had gone first; Charles was behind him, with the four other guards hemming him in. As Halloran reached the door of the lob-

by at the top of the aisle, he turned to face
Charles and performed an inexplicable panto-
mime. It was quite one second before Charles
realized that Halloran was tugging at his gun,
stuck in the holster.

The guard to the left of Charles softly said:
"Jesus!" and threw himself at Halloran as the
chief guard's gun came loose. There was a
rocket hiss and a dumdum roar, muffled.
There was another that crashed, unmuffled, a
yard from Charles' right ear. The two figures
at the head of the aisle collapsed limply and
the audience began to shriek. Somebody with
a very loud voice roared: "Keep calm! It's all
part of the play! Don't get panicky! It's part of
the play!"

The man who was roaring moved up to the
aisle door, fell silent, saw and smelled the
blood and fainted.

A woman began to pound the guard on
Charles' right with her fists, yelling: "What
did you do to my husband? You shot my husband!" She meant the man who had fainted;
Charles peeled her off the bodyguard.

Somehow they got into the lobby, followed
by most of the audience. The three bodyguards held them at bay. Charles found he
was deaf in his right ear and supposed it was
temporary. Least of his worries. Halloran had
taken a shot at him. The guard named Donnel
had shot Halloran down.

He said to Donnel: "You know Halloran
long?"

Donnel, not taking his eyes from the crowd,
said: "Couple of years, sir. He was just a guy

in the bodyguard pool."

"Get me out of here," Orsino said. "To the Syndic Building."

In the big black car, he could almost forget the horror; he could hope that time would erase it completely. It wasn't like polo. That shot had been *aimed*.

The limousine hissed to a halt before the titanic bulk of the Syndic Building, was checked and rolled on into the Unrestricted Entrance. An elevator silently lifted the car and passengers past floors devoted to Alcohol Clerical, Alcohol Research, and Testing Transport, Collections Audit and Control, Cleaning and Dyeing, Female Recruitment and Retirement up, up, up, past sections and subsections Charles had never entered, Syndic member though he was, to an automatic stop at a floor whose indicator said:

Enforcement and Public Relations

It was only 9:45 P.M.; F. W. Taylor would be in and working. Charles said: "Wait here, boys," and muttered the code phrase to the door. It sprang open.

F. W. Taylor was dictating, machine-gun fashion, to a mike. He looked dog-tired. His face turned up with a frown as Charles entered and then the frown became a beam of pleasure.

"Charles, my boy! Sit down!" He snapped off the machine.

"Uncle—" Charles began.

"It was so kind of you to drop in. I thought

you'd be at the theater."

"I was, Uncle, but—"

"I'm working on a revision for the next edition of *Organization, Symbolism and Morale.* You'd never guess who inspired it."

"I'm sure I wouldn't, Uncle. Uncle—"

"Old Thornberry, President of the Chase National. He had the infernal gall to refuse a line of credit to young McGurn. *Bankers!* You won't believe it, but people used to *beg* them to take over their property, tie up their incomes, virtually enslave them. People *demanded* it. The same way they demanded inexpensive liquor, tobacco and consumer goods, clean women and a chance to win a fortune; and our ancestors obliged them. Our ancestors were sneered at in their day, you know. They were called criminals when they distributed goods and services at a price people could afford to pay."

"Uncle!"

"Hush, boy, I know what you're going to say. You can't fool the people forever! When they'd had enough hounding and restriction, they rose in their might.

"The people demanded freedom of choice, Falcaro and the rest rose to lead them in the Syndic and the Mob, and they drove the Government into the sea."

"Uncle Frank—"

"From which it still occasionally ventures to annoy our coastal cities," F. W. Taylor commented. He warmed to his subject. "You should have seen the old boy blubber. The last of the old-time bankers, and they deserved

everything they got. They brought it on themselves. They had what they called *laissez-faire*,
and it worked for a while until they got to
tinkering with it. They demanded things
called protective tariffs, tax remissions,
subsidies—regulation, regulation, regulation,
always of the other fellow. But there were
enough bankers on all sides for everybody to
be somebody else's other fellow. Coercion
snowballed and the Government lost public
acceptance. They had a thing called the public
debt which I can't begin to explain to you except to say that it was something written on
paper and that it raised the cost of everything
tremendously. Well, believe me or not, they
didn't just throw away the piece of paper or
scratch out the writing on it. They let it ride
until ordinary people couldn't afford the
pleasant things in life."

"Uncle—"

A cautious periscope broke the choppy
water off Sea Island, Georgia. At the other end
of the periscope were Captain Van Dellen of
the North American Navy, lean as a hound,
and fat little Commander Grinnel.

"You might take her in a little closer, Van,"
said Grinnel mildly.

"The exercise won't do you any lasting
damage," Van Dellen said. Grinnel was very,
very near to a couple of admirals and normally Van Dellen gave him the kid-glove
treatment in spite of ranking him. But this
was *his* ship and no cloak-and-dagger artist
from an ONI desk was telling him how to con
it.

Grinnel smiled genially at the little joke. "I could call it a disguise," he said patting his paunch, "but you know me too well."

"You'll have no trouble with a sea like this," Van Dellen said, strictly business. He tried to think of some appropriate phrase to recognize the danger Grinnel was plunging into with no resources except quick wits, a trick ring and a pair of guns. But all that bubbled up to the top of his head was: Thank God I'm getting rid of this bastardly little Sociocrat. He'll kill me some day if he gets a clean shot and the chance of detection is zero. Thank God I'm a Constitutionist. We don't go in for things like that—or do we? Nobody ever tells me anything. A hack of a pigboat driver. And this little bastard's going to be an admiral some day. But that boy of mine'll be an admiral. He's brainy, like his mother.

Grinnel smiled and said: "Well, this would be it, wouldn't it?"

"Eh?" Van Dellen asked. "Oh. I see what you mean. Chuck!" he called a sailor. "Break out the Commander's capsule. Pass the word to stand by for ejection."

The Commander was fitted, puffing, into the capsule. He growled at the storekeeper: "You sure this thing was just unsealed? It feels sticky already."

A brash jaygee said: "I said it unsealed myself three minutes ago, Commander. It'll get stickier if we spend any more time talking. You have"—he glanced at his chronometer—"seventeen minutes now. Let me snap you in."

The Commander huddled down after a searching glance at the jaygee's face which photographed it forever in his memory. The top snapped down. Some day—some happy day—that squirt would very much regret telling him off. He gave an okay sign to Van Dellen who waved back meagerly and managed a smile. Three crewmen fitted the capsule into its lock.

Foomf!

It was through the hatch and bobbing on the surface. Its color matched the water's automatically. Grinnel waggled the lever that aimed it inshore and began to turn the propellor crank. He turned fast; the capsule—rudders, crank, flywheel, shaft and all—would dissolve in approximately fifteen minutes. It was his job to be ashore when that happened.

And ashore he'd be practically a free agent with the loosest sort of roving commission, until January 15. Then his orders became most specific.

THREE

Charles Orsino squirmed in the chair. "Uncle—" he pleaded.

"Yes," F. W. Taylor chuckled, "old Amadeo and his colleagues were called criminals. They were called bootleggers when they got liquor to people without worrying about the public debt or excise taxes. They were called smugglers when they sold switchblades in the South and cheap guns in the North. They were called counterfeiters when they sold cheap cigarettes and transportation tickets. They were called highjackers when they wrested goods from the normal inflation-ridden chain of middlemen and delivered them at a reasonable price to the consumers.

"They were criminals. Bankers were pillars of society.

"Yet these bankers who dominated society, who were considered the voice of eternal

truth when they spoke, who thought it was insanity to challenge their beliefs, started somewhere and perhaps they were the best thing
for their day and age that could be worked
out . . . ."

Father Ambrosius gnawed at a bit of salt
herring, wiped his hands, dug through the
litter in his chest and found a goose quill and
a page of parchment. He scrubbed vigorously
with a vinegar-soaked sponge at the writing on
the parchment and was pleased to see that it
came off nicely, leaving him a clean surface to
scribble his sermon notes on. He cut the quill
and slit it while waiting for the parchment to
dry, wondering idly what he had erased. (It
happened to be the last surviving copy of
Tacitus' *Annals*, VII, i-v.)

To work then. The sermon was to be
preached on Sexagesima Sunday, a prelude to
the solemn season of Lent. Father Ambrosius'
mind wandered in search of a text. Lent . . .
salt herring . . . penitence . . . the capital sins
. . . avarice . . . usury . . . delinquent pew rent
. . . fat-headed young Sir Baldwin in his tum-
bledown castle on the hill . . . salt herring
now and *per saeculae saeculorum* unless Sir
Baldwin paid up his delinquent pew rent.

At that moment, Sir Baldwin came swagger-
ing into the cell. Father Ambrosius rose courteously and said, with some insincerity: *"Pax
vobiscum."*

"Eh?" asked Sir Baldwin, his silly blue eyes
popping as he looked over his shoulder. "Oh,
you meant me, padre. It don't do a bit of good

to chatter at me in Latin, you know. The King's Norman is what I speak. I mean to say, if it's good enough for His Majesty Richard, it's good enough for me, what? Now, what can I do for you, padre?"

Father Ambrosius reminded him faintly: "You came to see me, Sir Baldwin."

"Eh? Oh. So I did. I was huntin' stag, padre, and I lost him after chasin' the whole morning, and what I want to know is, who's the right saint chap to ask for help in a pickle like that? I mean to say, I wanted to show the chaps some good sport and we started this beast and he got clean away. Don't misunderstand me, padre, they were good chaps and they didn't rot me about it, but that kind of talk gets about and doesn't do one a bit of good, what? So you tell me like a good fellow who's the right saint chap to put the matter in the best light for me?"

Father Ambrosius repressed an urge to grind his teeth, took thought and said: "St. Hubert, I believe, is interested in the stag hunt."

"Righto, padre! St. Hubert it is. Hubert, Hubert. I shan't forget it because I've a cousin named Hubert. Haven't seen him for years, poor old chap. He had the fistula—lived on slops and couldn't sit his horse for a day's huntin'. Poor old chap. Well, I'm off—no, there's another thing I wanted. Suppose this Sunday you preach a howlin' strong sermon against usury, what? That chap in the village, the goldsmith fellow, has the infernal gall to tell me I've got to give him Fallowfield! Forty acres, and he has the infernal gall to tell me they aren't mine any more. Be a good chap, padre, and sort of glare at him from the pulpit a few times to show him who you mean, what?"

"Usury *is* a sin," Father Ambrosius said cautiously, "but how does Fallowfield enter into it?"

Sir Baldwin twiddled the drooping ends of his limp, blond mustache with a trace of embarrassment. "Fact is, I told the chap when I borrowed the twenty marks that Fallowfield would stand as security. I ask you, padre, is it my fault that my tenants are a pack of lazy, thieving Saxon swine and I couldn't raise the money?"

The parish priest bristled unnoticeably. He was pure Saxon himself. "I shall do what I can," he said. "And Sir Baldwin, before you go—"

The young man stopped in the doorway and turned.

"Before you go, may I ask when we'll see your pew rent, to say nothing of the tithe?"

Sir Baldwin dismissed it with an airy wave of the hand. "I thought I just told you, padre. I haven't a farthing to my name and here's this chap in the village telling me to clear out of Fallowfield that I got from my father and his father before him. So how the devil—excuse me—can I pay rent and tithes and Peter's pence and all the other things you priest chaps expect from a man, what?" He held up his gauntleted hand as Father Ambrosius started to speak. "No, padre, not another

word about it. I know you'd love to tell me I
won't go to heaven if I act this way. I don't
doubt you're learned and all that, but I can
still tell you a thing or two, what? The fact is,
I *will* go to heaven. You see, padre, God's a
gentleman and he wouldn't bar another
gentleman over a trifle of money trouble that
could happen to any gentleman, now would
he?"

The fatuous beam was more than Father
Ambrosius could bear; his eyes fell.

"Righto," Sir Baldwin chirped. "And that
saint chap's name was St. Hubert. I didn't forget, see? Not quite the fool some people think
I am." And he was gone, whistling a recheat.

Father Ambrosius sat down again and
glared at the parchment. Preach a sermon on
usury for that popinjay. Well, usury *was* a sin.
Christians were supposed to lend to one
another in need and not count the cost or the
days. But who had ever heard of Sir Baldwin
ever lending anything? Of course, he was lord
of the manor and protected you against in-
vasion, but there didn't seem to be any
invasions any more . . . .

Wearily, the parish priest dipped his pen
and scratched on the parchment: ROM. XIII
ii, viii, XV i. "Whosoever resisteth the power
resisteth the ordinance of God . . . owe no
man any thing . . . we that are strong ought to
bear the infirmities of the weak . . . ." A triple-
plated text, which, reinforced by a brow of
thunder from the pulpit, should make the
village goldsmith think twice before pressing
his demand on Sir Baldwin. Usury *was* a sin.

There was a different knock on the doorframe.

The goldsmith, a leather-aproned fellow named John, stood there twisting his cap in his big, burn-scarred hands.

"Yes, my son? Come in." But he scowled at the fellow involuntarily. He should know better than to succumb to the capital sin of avarice. "Well, what is it?"

"Father," the fellow said, "I've come to give you this." He passed a soft leather purse to the priest. It clinked.

Father Ambrosius emptied it on his desk and stirred the broad silver coins wonderingly with his finger. Five marks and eleven silver pennies. No more salt herring until Lent! Silver forwarded to his bishop in an amount that would do credit to the parish! A gilding job for the image of the Blessed Virgin! Perhaps glass panes in one or two of the church windows!

And then he stiffened and swept the money back into the purse. "You got this by sin," he said flatly. "The sin of avarice worked in your heart and you practiced the sin of usury on your fellow Christians. Don't give this money to the Church; give it back to your victims."

"Father," the fellow said, nearly blubbering, "excuse me but you don't understand! They come to me and come to me. They say it's all right with them, that they're hiring the money the way you'd hire a horse. Doesn't that make sense? Do you think I *wanted* to become a moneylender? No! I was an honest goldsmith and an honest goldsmith can't help himself. All the money in the village drifts somehow into his hands. One leaves a mark with you for safekeeping and pays you a penny the year to guard it. Another brings you silver coins to make into a basin, and you get to keep whatever coins are left over. And then others come to you and say 'Let me have soandso's mark to use for a year and then I'll pay it back and with it another mark.' Father, they beg me! They say they'll be ruined if I don't lend to them, their old parents will die if they can't fee the leech, or their dead will roast forever unless they can pay for Masses and what's a man to *do?*"

"Sin no more," the priest answered simply. It was no problem.

The fellow was getting angry. "Very well for you to sit there and say so, Father. But what do you think paid for the Masses you said for the repose of Goodie Howat's soul? And how did Tom the Thatcher buy his wagon so he could sell his beer in Glastonbury at a better price? And how did farmer Major hire the men from Wealing to get in his hay before the great storm could ruin it? And a hundred things more. I tell you, this parish would be a worse place without John Goldsmith and he doesn't propose to be pointed at any longer as a black sinner! I didn't want to fall into usury but I did, and *when* I did, I found out that those who hoist their noses highest at the moneylender when they pass him in the road are the same ones who beg the hardest when they come to his shop for a loan!"

The priest was stunned by the outburst.

John seemed honest, the facts were the facts
—can good come out of evil? And there were
stories that His Holiness the Pope himself had
certain dealings with the Langobards—bench-
ers, or bankers or whatever they called themselves . . . .

"I must think on this, my son," he said.
"Perhaps I was overhasty. Perhaps in the days
of St. Paul usury was another thing entirely.
Perhaps what you practice is not *really* usury
but merely something that resembles it. You
may leave this silver with me."

When John left, Father Ambrosius squeezed
his eyes tight shut and pressed the knuckles
of both hands to his forehead. Things *did*
change. Under the dispensation of the Old
Testament, men had more wives than one.
That was sinful now, but surely Abraham,
Isaac and Jacob were in heaven? Paul wrote
his epistles to the little islands of Christians
surrounded by seas of pagans. Surely in those
days it was necessary for Christians to be
bound closely together against the common
enemy, whereas in these modern times, the
ties could be safely relaxed a trifle? How
could sinning have paid for the repose of
Goodie Howat's soul, got a better price for
brewer Thatcher's ale and saved the village
hay crop? The devil was tricky, but not *that*
tricky, surely. A few more such tricks and the
parish would resemble the paradise terres-
trial!

Father Ambrosius dashed from his study to
the altar of the little stone church and began
furiously to turn the pages of the huge metal-
bound lectern Bible.

"For the love of money is the root of all evil—"

It burst on Father Ambrosius with a great light that the words of Paul were in reference not to *John Goldsmith's* love of money but to *Sir Baldwin's* love of money.

He dashed back to his study and his pen began to squeak over the parchment, obliterating the last dim trace of Tacitus' *Annals*, VII, i-v. The sermon would be a scorcher, all right, but it wouldn't scorch John Goldsmith. It would scorch Sir Baldwin for ruthlessly and against the laws of God and man refusing to turn Fallowfield over to the moneylender. There would be growls of approval in the church that Sunday, and many black looks directed against Sir Baldwin for his attempt to bilk the parish's friend and benefactor, the moneylender.

"And that," F. W. Taylor concluded, chuckling, "is how power passes from one pair of hands to another, and how public acceptance of the change follows on its heels. A strange thing—people always think that each exchange of power is the last that will ever take place."

He seemed to be finished.

"Uncle," Orsino said, "somebody tried to kill me."

Taylor stared at him for a long minute, speechless. "What happened?" he finally asked.

"I went formal to the theater, with five bodyguards. The chief guard, name of Halloran, took a shot at me. One of my boys got in the way. He was killed."

Taylor's fingers began to play a tattoo on his annunciator board. Faces leaped into existence on its various screens as he fired orders. "Charles Orsino's chief bodyguard for tonight —Halloran. Trace him. The works. He tried to kill Orsino. Same on the rest of his guards for the night."

He clicked off the board switches and turned grimly to Orsino. "Now you," he said. "What have *you* been up to?"

"Just doing my job, Uncle," Orsino said uneasily.

"Still bagman at the 101st?"

"Yes."

"Fooling with any women?"

"Nothing special, Uncle. Nothing intense."

"Disciplined or downgraded anybody lately?"

"Certainly not. The precinct runs like a watch. I'll match their morale against any outfit east of the Mississippi. Why are you taking this so heavy?"

"Because you're the third. The other two— your cousin Thomas McGurn and your uncle Robert Orsino—didn't have guards to get in the way. One other question."

"Yes, Uncle."

"My boy, *why* didn't you tell me about this when you first came in?"

FOUR

A family council was called the next day. Orsino, very much a junior, had never been admitted to one before. He knew why the exception was being made, and didn't like the reason.

Edward Falcaro wagged his formidable white beard at the thirty-odd Syndic chiefs around the table and growled: "I think we'll dispense with reviewing production and so on. I want to talk about this damn gunplay. Dick, bring us up to date."

He lit a vile cigar and leaned back.

Richard W. Reiner rose. "Thomas McGurn," he said, "frapped April 15 in his private dining room at the Astor. Elsie Warshofsky, his waitress, must be considered the principal suspect, but—"

Edward Falcaro snapped: "Suspect, hell! She killed him, didn't she?"

"I was about to say, but the evidence so far is merely cumulative. Mrs. Warshofsky jumped—fell—or was pushed—from the dining-room window. The weapon was found beside the window. There are no known witnesses. Mrs. Warshofsky's history presents no unusual features. An acquaintance submitted a statement — based, she frankly admitted, on nothing definite—that Mrs. Warshofsky sometimes talked in a way that led her to wonder if she might not be a member of the secret terrorist organization known as the D.A.R. In this connection, it should be noted that Mrs. Warshofsky's maiden name was Adams.

"Robert Orsino, killed April 21 by a napalm grenade concealed in his pillow and fused with a pressure-sensitive switch. His valet, Edward Blythe, disappeared from view. He was picked up April 23 by a posse on the beach at Montauk Point, but died before he could be questioned. Examination of his stomach contents showed a lethal quantity of sodium fluoride. It is presumed that the poison was self-administered."

"Presumed!" the old man snorted, and puffed out a lethal quantity of cigar smoke.

"Blythe's history," Reiner went on blandly, "presents no unusual features. It should be noted that a commerce-raider of the so-called North American Government Navy was reported off Montauk Point during the night of April 23-24 by local residents.

"Charles Orsino, attacked April 30 by his bodyguard James Halloran in the lobby of the Costello Memorial Theater. Halloran fired one shot which killed another bodyguard and was then himself killed. Halloran's history presents no unusual features except that he had a considerable interest in—uh—history. He collected and presumably read obsolete books dealing with pre-Syndic, pre-Mob America. Investigators found by his bedside the first volume of a work published in 1942 called *The Growth of the American Republic* by Morison and Commager. It was opened to Chapter Ten, 'The War of Independence.'"

Reiner took his seat.

F. W. Taylor said dryly: "Dick, did you forget to mention that Warshofsky, Blythe and Halloran are known officers of the N.A. Navy?"

Reiner said: "You are being facetious. Are you implying that I have omitted pertinent facts?"

"I'm implying that you artistically stacked the deck. With a rumor, a dubious commerce-raider report and a note on a man's hobby, you want us to sweep the dastards from the sea, don't you—just the way you always have?"

"I am not ashamed of my expressed attitude on the question of the so-called North American Government and will defend it at any proper time and place."

"Shut the hell up, you two," Edward Falcaro growled. "I'm trying to think." He thought for perhaps half a minute and then looked up, baffled. "Has anybody got any ideas?"

Charles Orsino cleared his throat, amazed at his own temerity. The old man's eyebrows shot up, but he grudgingly said: "I guess you can say something, since they thought you were important enough to shoot."

Orsino said: "Maybe it's some outfit over in Europe or Asia?"

Edward Falcaro asked: "Anybody know anything about Europe or Asia? Jimmy, you flew over once, didn't you? To see about Anatolian poppies when the Mob had trouble with Mex labor?"

Jimmy Falcaro said creakily: "Yeah. It was a waste of time. They have these little dirt farmers scratching out just enough food for the family and maybe raising a quarter-acre of poppy. That's *all* there is from the China Sea to the Mediterranean. In England— Frank, you tell 'em. You explained it to me once."

Taylor rose. "The forests came back to England. When finance there lost its morale and couldn't hack its way out of the paradoxes, that was the end. When that happens you've got to have a large, virile criminal class ready to take over and do the work of distribution and production. Maybe some of you know how the English were. The poor buggers had civilized all the illegality out of the stock. They couldn't do anything that wasn't respectable. From sketchy reports, I gather that England is now forest and a few thousand starving people. One fellow says the men still wear derbies and stagger to their offices in the City.

"France is peasants, drunk three-quarters of the time.

"Russia is peasants, drunk *all* the time.

"Germany—well, there the criminal class was *too* big and *too* virile. The place is a cemetery."

He shrugged: "Say it, somebody. The Mob's gunning for us."

Reiner jumped to his feet. "I will *never* support such a hypothesis!" he shrilled. "It is *mischievous* to imply that a century of peace has been ended, that our three-thousand-mile border with our friend to the West—"

Taylor intoned satirically: *"Un*-blemished, my friends, by a *single* for-ti-fi-*ca*-tion—"

Edward Falcaro yelled: "Stop your damn foolishness, Frank Taylor! This is no laughing matter."

Taylor snapped: "Have you been in Mob Territory lately?"

"I have," the old man said. He scowled. "How'd you like it?"

Edward Falcaro shrugged irritably. "They have their ways, we have ours. The Regan line is running thin, but we're not going to forget that Jimmy Regan stood shoulder to shoulder with Amadeo Falcaro in the old days. There's such a thing as loyalty."

F. W. Taylor said: "There's such a thing as blindness."

He had gone too far. Edward Falcaro rose from his chair and leaned forward, bracing himself on the table. He said flatly: "This is a statement, gentlemen. I won't pretend I'm happy about the way things are in Mob Territory. I won't pretend I think old man Regan is a balanced, dependable person. I won't pre-

tend I think the Mob clients are enjoying anywhere near the service that Syndic clients
enjoy. I'm perfectly aware that on our visits of
state to Mob Territory we see pretty much
what our hosts want us to see. But I cannot
believe that any group which is rooted on the
principles of freedom and service can have
gone very wrong.

"Maybe I'm mistaken, gentlemen. But I
cannot believe that a descendant of Jimmy
Regan would order a descendant of Amadeo
Falcaro murdered. We will consider every
other possibility first. Frank, is that clear?"

"Yes," Taylor said.

"All right," Edward Falcaro grunted. "Now
let's go about this thing systematically. Dick,
you go right down the line with the charge
that the Government's responsible for these
atrocities. I hate to think that myself. If they
are, we're going to have to spend a lot of time
and trouble hunting them down and doing
something about it. As long as they stick to a
little commerce-raiding and a few coastal
attacks, I can't say I'm really unhappy about
them. They don't do much harm, and they
keep us on our toes and—maybe this one is
most important—they keep our clients'
memories of the bad old days that we delivered them from alive. That's a great deal to
surrender for the doubtful pleasures of a
long, expensive campaign. If assassination's
in the picture I suppose we'll have to knock
them off—but we've got to be *sure*."

"May I speak?" Reiner asked icily.

The old man nodded and relit his cigar.

"I have been called—behind my back, naturally—a fanatic," Reiner said. He pointedly did not look anywhere near F. W. Taylor as he spoke the word. "Perhaps this is correct and perhaps fanaticism is what's needed at a time like this. Let me point out what the so-called Government stands for: brutal 'taxation,' extirpation of gambling, denial of life's simple pleasures to the poor and severe limitation of them to all but the wealthy, sexual prudery viciously enforced by penal laws of appalling barbarity, endless regulation and coercion governing every waking minute of the day. That was its record during the days of its power and that would be its record if it returned to power. I fail to see how this menace to our liberty can be condoned by certain marginal benefits which are claimed to accrue from its continued existence." He faltered for a moment as his face twisted with an unpleasant memory. In a lower, unhappier voice, he went on: "I—I was alarmed the other day by something I overheard. Two small children were laying bets at the Kiddy Counter of the horse-room I frequent, and I stopped on my way to the hundred-carlo window for a moment to hear their childish prattle. They were doping the forms for the sixth at Hialeah, I believe, when one of them digressed to say: 'My mommy doesn't play the horses. She thinks all the horse-rooms should be closed.'

"It wrung my heart, gentlemen, to hear that. I wanted to take that little boy aside and tell him: 'Son, your mommy doesn't have to play the horses. Nobody has to play the horses unless he wants to. But as long as one single person wants to lay a bet on a horse and another person is willing to take it, nobody has the right to say the horse-rooms should be closed.' Naturally I did not take the little boy aside and tell him that. It would have been an impractical approach to the problem. The *practical* approach is the one I have always advocated and still do. Strike at the heart of the infection! Destroy the remnants of Government and cauterize the wound so that it will never reinfect again. Nor is my language too strong. When I realize that the mind of an innocent child has been corrupted so that he will prattle that the liberties of his brothers must be infringed on, that their harmless pleasures must be curtailed, my blood runs cold and I call it what it is: *treason.*"

Orsino had listened raptly to the words and joined in a burst of spontaneous applause that swept around the table. He had never had a brush with Government himself and he hardly believed in the existence of the shadowy, terrorist D.A.R., but Reiner had made it sound so near and menacing!

But Uncle Frank was on his feet. "We seem to have strayed from the point," he said dryly. "For anybody who needs his memory refreshed, I'll state that the point is two assassinations and one near miss. I fail to see the connection, if any, with Dick Reiner's paranoid delusions of persecution. I especially fail to see the revelance of the word 'treason.' Treason to what—us? The Syndic is not a government. It must not become enmeshed in the symbols and folklore of a government or it will be first chained and then strangled by them. The Syndic is an organization of high morale and easygoing, hedonistic personality. The fact that it succeeded the Government occurred because the Government had become an organization of low morale and inflexible, puritanic, sado-masochistic personality. I have no illusions about the Syndic lasting forever, and I hope nobody else here has. Naturally I want it to last our lifetime, my children's lifetime, and as long after that as I can visualize my descendants, but don't think I have any burning affection for my unborn great-great grandchildren. Now, if there is anybody here who doesn't want it to last that long, I suggest to him that the quickest way to demoralize the Syndic is to adopt Dick Reiner's proposal of a holy war for a starter. From there we can proceed to an internal heresy hunt, a census, excise taxes, income taxes and wars of aggression. Now, what about getting back to the assassinations?"

Orsino shook his head, thoroughly confused by now. But the confusion vanished as a girl entered the room, whispered something in the ear of Edward Falcaro and sat down calmly by his side. He wasn't the only one who noticed her. Most of the faces there registered surprise and some indignation. The Syndic had a very strong tradition of masculinity.

Edward Falcaro ignored the surprise and

indignation. He said placidly: "That was very interesting, Frank, what I understood of it. But it's always interesting when I go ahead and do something because it's the smart thing to do, and then listen to you explain my reasons—including fifty or sixty that never crossed my mind."

There was a laugh around the table that Charles Orsino thought was unfair. He knew, Edward Falcaro knew, and everybody knew that Taylor credited Falcaro with sound intuitive judgment rather than analytic power. He supposed the old man—intuitively—had decided a laugh was needed to clear the air of the quarrel and irrelevance.

Falcaro went on: "The way things stand now, gentlemen, we don't know very much, do we?" He bit a fresh cigar and lighted it meditatively. From a cloud of rank smoke he said: "So the thing to do is find out more, isn't it?" In spite of the beard and the cigar, there was something of a sly, teasing child about him. "So what do you say to slipping one of our own people into the Government to find out whether they're dealing in assassination or not?"

Charles Orsino alone was näive enough to speak; the rest knew that the old man had something up his sleeve. Charles said: "You can't do it, sir! They have lie-detectors and drugs and all sorts of things—" His voice died down miserably under Falcaro's too benign smile and the looks of irritation verging on disgust from the rest. The enigmatic girl scowled. *God damn them all!* Charles thought, sinking into his chair and wishing he could sink into the earth.

"The young man," Falcaro said blandly, "speaks the truth—no less true for being somewhat familiar to us all. But what if we have a way to get around the drugs and lie-detectors, gentlemen? Which of you bold fellows would march into the jaws of death by joining the Government, spying on them and trying to report back?"

Charles stood up, prudence and timidity washed away by a burning need to make up for his embarrassment with a grandstand play. "I'll go, sir," he said very calmly. *And if I get killed that'll show 'em; then they'll be sorry.*

"Good boy," Edward Falcaro said briskly, with a well-that's-that air. "The young lady here will take care of you."

Charles steadily walked down the long room to the head of the table, thinking that he must be cutting a rather fine figure. Uncle Frank ruined his exit by catching his sleeve and halting him as he passed his seat. "Good luck, Charles," Uncle Frank whispered. "And for Christ's sake, keep a better guard up. Can't you see the old devil planned it this way from the beginning?"

"Good-by, Uncle Frank," Charles said, suddenly feeling quite sick as he walked on. The young lady rose and opened the door for him. She was graceful as a cat, and a conviction overcame Charles Orsino that he was the canary.

FIVE

Max Wyman shoved his way through such a roar of voices and such a crush of bodies as he had never known before. Scratch Sheet Square was bright as day—brighter. Atomic lamps, mounted on hundred-story buildings hosed and squirted the happy mob with blue-white glare. The Scratch Sheet's moving sign was saying in fiery letters seventy-five feet tall: "11:58 PM EST...DECEMBER 31... COPS SAY TWO MILLION JAM NYC STREETS TO GREET NEW YEAR...11:59 PM EST...DECEMBER 31...FALCARO JOKES ON TV 'NEVER THOUGHT WE'D MAKE IT'...12:00 MIDNIGHT JANUARY 1...HAPPY NEW YEAR..."

The roar of voices had become insane. Max Wyman held his head, hating it, hating them all, trying to shut them out. Half a dozen young men against whom he was jammed were tearing the clothes off a girl. They were laughing and she was too, making only a pretense of defending herself. It was one of New York's mild winter nights. Wyman looked at the white skin not knowing that his eyes gloated. He yelled curses at her, and the young men. But nobody heard his whisky-hoarsened young voice.

Somebody thrust a bottle at him and made mouths, trying to yell: "Happy New Year!" He grabbed feverishly at the bottle and held it to his mouth, letting the liquor gurgle once, twice, three times. Then the bottle was snatched away, not by the man who had passed it to him. A hilarious fat woman plastered herself against Wyman and kissed him clingingly on the mouth, to his horror and disgust. She was torn away from him by a laughing, white-haired man and turned willingly to kissing him instead.

Two strapping girls jockeyed Wyman between them and began to tear *his* clothes off, laughing at their switcheroo on the year's big gag. He clawed out at them hysterically and they stopped, the laughter dying on their lips as they saw his look of terrified rage. A sudden current in the crowd parted Wyman from them; another bottle bobbed on the sea of humanity. He clutched at it and this time did not drink. He stuffed it hurriedly under the waistband of his shorts and kept a hand on it as the eddy of humanity bore him on to the fringes of the roaring mob.

"SYNDIC LEADERS HAIL NEW YEAR . . . TAYLOR PRAISES CENTURY OF FREEDOM

. . . 12:05 AM EST JANUARY 1 . . ."

Wyman was mashed up against a girl who
first smiled at his young face invitingly . . .
and then looked again. "Get away from me!"
she shrieked, pounding on his chest with her
small fists. You could hear individual voices
now, but the crowd was still dense. She kept
screaming at him and hitting him until suddenly Scratch Sheet Square Upramp loomed
and the crowd fizzed onto it like uncorked
champagne, Wyman and the screaming girl
carried along the moving plates underfoot.
The crowd boiled onto the northbound strip,
relieving the crush; the girl vanished, whimpering, into the mob.

Wyman, rubbing his ear mechanically,
shuffled with downcast eyes to the eastbound
ramp and collapsed onto a bench gliding by at
five miles per hour. He looked stupidly at the
ten-mile and fifteen-mile strips, but did not
dare step onto them. He had been drinking
steadily for a month. He would fall and the
bottle would break.

He lurched off the five-mile strip at Riveredge Downramp. Nobody got off with him.
Riveredge was a tangle of freightways over,
under, and on the surface. He worked there.

Wyman picked his way past throbbing conveyors roofed against pilferage, under gurg-
ling fuel and water and waste pipes, around
vast metal warehouses and storage tanks. It
was not dark or idle in Riveredge. Twenty-
four hours was little enough time to bring
Manhattan its daily needs and carry off its
daily waste and manufacturers. Under day-

light atomics the transport engineers in their glass perches read the dials and turned the switches. Breakdown crews scurried out from emergency stations as bells clanged, to replace a sagging plate, remag a failing ehrenhafter, unplug a jam of nylon bales at a too-sharp corner.

He found Breakdown Station 26, hitched his jacket over the bottle and swayed in, drunk enough to think he could pretend he was sober. "Hi," he said hoarsely to the shift foreman. "Got jammed up in the celebration."

"We heard it clear over here," the foreman said, looking at him closely. "Are you all right, Max?"

The question enraged him. "'Smatter?" he yelled. "Had a couple, sure. Think 'm drunk? Tha' wha' ya think?"

"Jesus," the foreman said wearily. "Look, Max, I can't send you out tonight. You might get killed. I'm trying to be reasonable and I wish you'd do as much for me. What's biting you, boy? Nobody has anything against a few drinks and a few laughs. I went on a bender last month myself. But you get so God-damned *mean* I can't stand you and neither can anybody else."

Wyman spewed obscenity at him and tried to swing on him. He was surprised and filled with self-pity when somebody caught his arm and somebody else caught his other arm. It was Dooley and Weintraub, his shiftmates, looking unhappy and concerned.

"Lousy rats!" Wyman choked out. "Leas' a man's buddies c'd do is back'm up . . . ." He began to cry, hating them, and then fell asleep on his feet. Dooley and Weintraub eased him down onto the floor.

The foreman mopped his head and appealed to Dooley: "He always like this?" He had been transferred to Station 26 only two weeks before.

Dooley shrugged. "You might say so. He showed up about three months ago. Said he used to be a breakdown man in Buffalo, on the yards. He knew the work all right. But I never saw such a mean kid. Never a good word for anybody. Never any fun. Booze, booze, booze. This time he really let go."

Weintraub said unexpectedly: "I think he's what they used to call an alcoholic."

"What the hell's that?" the foreman demanded.

"I read about it. It's something they used to have before the Syndic. I read about it. Things were a lot different then. People picking on you all the time, everybody mad all the time. The girls were scared to give it away and the boys were scared to take it—but they did it anyway and it was kind of like fighting with yourself *inside* yourself. The fighting wore some people out so much they just couldn't take it any more. Instead of going on benders for a change of pace like sensible people, they boozed *all* the time—and they had a fight inside themselves about *that* so they boozed harder." He looked defensive at their skeptical faces. "I *read* it," he insisted.

"Well," the foreman said inconclusively, "I heard things used to be pretty bad. Did these alcoholers get over it?"

"I don't know," Weintraub admitted. "I didn't read that far."

"Hm. I think I'd better can him." The foreman was studying their faces covertly, hoping to read a reaction. He did. Both the men looked relieved. "Yeh. I think I'd better can him. He can go to the Syndic for relief if he has to. He doesn't do us much good here. Put some soup on and get it down him when he wakes up." The foreman, an average kindly man, hoped the soup would help.

But at about three-thirty, after two trouble calls in succession, they noticed that Wyman had left the station leaving no word.

The fat little man struggled out of the New Year's Eve throng; he had been caught by accident. Commander Grinnel did not go in for celebrations. When he realized that January 15 was now fifteen days away, he doubted that he would ever celebrate again. It was a two-man job he had to do on the fifteenth, and so far he had not found the other man.

He rode the sidewalk to Columbia Square. He had been supplied with a minimum list of contacts. One had moved, and in the crazily undisciplined Syndic Territory it was impossible to trace anybody. Another had died—of too much morphine. Another had beaten her husband almost to death with a chair leg and was in custody awaiting trial. The Commander wondered briefly and querulously: Why do we always have such unstable people here? Or does that bastard Emory deliberately saddle me with them when I'm on a mission? Wouldn't put it past him.

The final contact on the list was a woman. She'd be worthless for the business of January 15; that called for some physical strength, some technical knowledge, and a residual usefulness to the Government. Professor Speiser had done some good work here on industrial sabotage, but taken away from the scene of possible operations, she'd just be a millstone. He had his record to think of.

Sabotage—

If a giggling threesome hadn't been looking his way from a bench across the sidewalk, he would have ground his teeth. In recent weeks, he had done what he estimated as an easy three million carlos worth of damage to Syndic Territory industry. And the stupid sons of bitches hadn't *noticed* it! Repair crews had rebuilt the fallen walls, mechanics had tut-tutted over the wrecked engines and replaced them, troubleshooters had troubleshot the scores of severed communications lines and fuel mains.

He had hung around.

"Sam, you see this? Melted through, like with a little thermite bomb. How in the hell did a thing like that happen?"

"I don't know. I wasn't here. Let's get it fixed, kid."

"Okay . . . you think we ought to report this to somebody?"

"If you want to. I'll mention it to Larry. But I don't see what he can do about it. Must've been some kids. You gotta put it down as fair wear and tear. Boys will be boys."

Remembering, he did grind his teeth. But

they were at Columbia Square.

Professor Speiser lived in one of the old plastic brick faculty houses. Her horsy face, under a curling net, looked out of the annunciator plate. "Yes? What is it?"

"Professor Speiser, I believe you know my daughter, Miss *Freeman*. She asked me to look you up while I was in New York. Have I come much too late?"

"Oh, dear. Why, no. I suppose not. Come in, Mr.—Mr. Freeman."

In her parlor, she faced him apprehensively. When she spoke she rolled out her sentences like the lecturer she was. "Mr. Freeman—as I suppose you'd prefer me to call you —you asked a moment ago whether you'd come too late. I realize that the question was window dressing, but my answer is quite serious. You have come too late. I have decided to dissociate myself from—let us say, from your daughter, Miss Freeman."

The Commander asked only: "Is that irrevocable?"

"Quite. It wouldn't be fair of me to ask you to leave without an explanation. I am perfectly willing to give one. I realize now that my friendship with Miss Freeman and the work I did for her stemmed from, let us say a certain vacancy in my life."

He looked at a picture on her desk of a bald, pleasant-faced fellow with a pipe.

She followed his eyes and said with a sort of shy pride: "That is Dr. Mordecai, of the University's Faculty of Dentistry. Like myself, a long-time celibate. We plan to marry."

The Commander said: "Do you feel that Dr. Mordecai might like to meet my daughter?"

"No. I do not. We expect to have very little time for outside activities, between our professional careers and our personal lives. Please don't misunderstand, Mr. Freeman. I am still your daughter's friend. I always shall be. But somehow I no longer find in myself an urgency to express the friendship. It seems like a beautiful dream—and a quite futile one. I have come to realize that one can live a full life without Miss Freeman. Now, it's getting quite late—"

He smiled ruefully and rose. "May I wish you every happiness, Professor Speiser?" he said, extending his hand.

She beamed with relief. "I was so afraid you'd—"

Her face went limp and she stood swaying drunkenly as the needle in the ring popped her skin.

The Commander, his face as dead as hers, disconnected his hand and sheathed the needle carefully again. He drew one of his guns, shot her through the heart and walked out of the apartment.

Old fool! She should have known better.

Max Wyman stumbled through the tangle of Riveredge, his head a pot of molten lead and his legs twitching under him as he fled from his shame.

Dimly, as if with new eyes, he saw that he was not alone. Riveredge was technically uninhabited. Then what voices called guardedly to him from the shadows: "Buddy—buddy— wait up a minute, buddy—did you score? Did you score?"

He lurched on and the voices became bolder. The snaking conveyors and ramps sliced out sectors of space. Storage tanks merged with inflow mains to form sheltered spots where they met. No spot was without its whining, appealing voice. He stood at last, quivering, leaning against a gigantic I-beam that supported a heavy-casting freightway. A scrap sheet of corrugated iron rested against the bay of the I-beam, and the sheet quivered and fell outward. An old man's voice said: "You're beat, son. Come on in."

He staggered a step forward and collapsed on a pallet of rags as somebody carefully leaned the sheet back into place again.

SIX

Max Wyman woke raving with the chuck horrors. There was somebody there to hand him candy bars, sweet lemonade, lump sugar. There was somebody to shove him easily back into the pallet of rags when he tried to stumble forth in a hunt for booze. On the second day he realized that it was an old man whose face looked gray and paralyzed. His name was T. G. Pendelton, he said.

After a week, he let Max Wyman take little walks about their part of Riveredge—but not by night. "We've got some savage people here," he said. "They'd murder you for a pint. The women are worst. If one calls to you, don't go. You'll wind up dumped through a manhole into the Hudson. Poor folk."

"You're *sorry* for them?" Wyman asked, startled. It was a new idea to him. Since Buffalo, he had never been sorry for anybody. Something awful had happened there, some terrible betrayal . . . he passed his bony hand across his forehead. He didn't want to think about it.

"Would I live here if I weren't?" T. G. asked him. "Sometimes I can help them. There's nobody else to help them. They're old and sick and they don't fit anywhere. That's why they're savage. You're young—the only young man I've ever seen in Riveredge. There's so much outside for the young. But when you get old it sometimes throws you."

"The God-damned Syndic," Wyman snarled, full of hate.

T. G. shrugged. "Maybe it's too easy for sick old people to get booze. They lose somebody they spent a life with and it throws them. People harden into a pattern. They always had fun, they think they always will. Then half of the pattern's gone and they can't stand it, some of them. You got it early. What was the ringing bell?"

Wyman collapsed into the bay of the I-beam as if he'd been kicked in the stomach. A wave of intolerable memory swept over him. A ringing bell, a wobbling pendulum, a flashing light, the fair face of his betrayer, the hateful one of Hogan, stirred together in a hell brew. "Nothing," he said hoarsely, thinking that he'd give his life for enough booze to black him out. "Nothing."

"You kept talking about it," T. G. said. "Was it real?"

"It couldn't have been," Wyman muttered. "There aren't such things. No. There was her and that Syndic and that bastard Hogan. I don't want to talk about it."

"Suit yourself."

He did talk about it later, curiously clouded though it was. The years in Buffalo. The violent love affair with Inge. The catastrophic scene when he found her with Hogan, kingpin of the Syndic. The way he felt turned inside-out, the lifetime of faith in the Syndic behind him and the lifetime of a faith in Inge ahead of him, both wrecked, the booze, the flight from Buffalo to Erie, to Pittsburgh, to Tampa, to New York. And somehow, insistently, the ringing bell, the wobbling pendulum and the flashing light that kept intruding between episodes of reality.

T. G. listened patiently, fed him, hid him when infrequent patrols went by. T. G. never told him his own story, but a bloated woman who lived with a yellow-toothed man in an abandoned storage tank did one day, her voice echoing from the curving, windowless walls of corrugated plastic. She said T.G. had been an alky chemist, reasonably prosperous, reasonably happy, reasonably married. His wife was the faithful kind and he was not. With unbelievable slyness she had dulled the pain for years with booze and he had never suspected. Then she had killed herself after one frightful week-long debauch in Riveredge. T. G. came down to Riveredge for the body and returned after giving it burial and drawing his savings from the bank. He had never left Riveredge since.

"Worsh'p the groun' that man walks on," the bloated woman mumbled. "Nev' gets mad, nev' calls you hard names. Give y'a bottle if y' need it. Talk to y' if y' blue. Worsh'p that man.''

Max Wyman walked from the storage tank, sickened. T. G.'s charity covered that creature and him.

It was the day he told T. G.: "I'm getting out of here."

The gray, paralyzed-looking face almost smiled. "See a man first?"

"Friend of yours?"

"Somebody who heard about you. Maybe he can do something for you. He feels the way you do about the Syndic."

Wyman clenched his teeth. The pain still came at the thought. Syndic, Hogan, Inge and betrayal. God, to be able to hit back at them!

The red tide ebbed. Suddenly he stared at T. G. and demanded: "Why? Why should you put me in touch? What is this?"

T. G. shrugged. "I don't worry about the Syndic. I worry about people. I've been worrying about you. You're a little insane, Max, like all of us here."

"God damn you!"

"He has . . ."

Max Wyman paused a long time and said: "Go on, will you?" He realized that anybody else would have apologized. But he couldn't and he knew that T. G. knew he couldn't.

The old man said: "A little insane. Bottled-up hatred. It's better out of you than in. It's better to sock the man you hate and stand a chance of having him sock you back than it is just to hate him and let the hate gnaw you like a graveworm."

"What've you got against the Syndic?"

"Nothing, Max. Nothing against it and nothing for it. What I'm for is people. The Syndic is people. You're people. Slug 'em if you want and they'll have a chance to slug you back. Maybe you'll pull down the Syndic like Samson in the temple; more likely it'll crush you. But you'll be *doing* something about it. That's the great thing. That's the thing people have to learn—or they wind up in Riveredge."

"You're crazy."

"I told you I was, or I wouldn't be here."

The man came at sunset. He was short and pudgy, with a halo of wispy hair and the coldest, grimmest eyes that Wyman had ever seen. He shook hands with Wyman, and the young man noted simultaneously a sharp pain in his finger and that the stranger wore an elaborate gold ring. Then the world got hazy and confused. He had a sense that he was being asked questions, that he was answering them, that it went on for hours and hours.

When things quite suddenly came into focus again, the pudgy man was saying: "I can introduce myself now. Commander Grinnel, of the North American Navy. My assignment is recruiting. The preliminary examination has satisfied me that you are no plant and would be a desirable citizen of the N. A. Government. I invite you to join us."

"What would I do?" Wyman asked steadily.

"That depends on your aptitudes. What do you think you would like to do?"

Wyman said: "Kill me some Syndics."

The Commander stared at him with those cold eyes. He said at last: "It can probably be arranged. Come with me."

They went by train to Cape Cod. At midnight on January 15, the Commander and Wyman left their hotel room and strolled about the streets. The Commander taped small packets to the four legs of the microwave relay tower that connected Cape Cod with the Continental Press common-carrier circuits and taped other packets to the police station's motor pool gate.

At 1:00 A.M., the tower exploded and the motor pool gate fused into an impassable puddle of blue-hot molten metal. Simultaneously, fifty men in turtleneck sweaters and caps appeared from nowhere on Center Street. Half of them barricaded the street, firing on citizens and cops who came too close. The others systematically looted every store between the barricade and the beach.

Blinking a laser flash in code, the Commander approached the deadline unmolested and was let through with Wyman at his heels. The goods, the raiders, the Commander and Wyman were aboard a submarine by 2:35 and under way ten minutes later.

After Commander Grinnel had exchanged congratulations with the sub commander, he presented Wyman.

"A recruit. Normally I wouldn't have bothered, but he had a rather special motivation. He could be very useful."

The sub commander studied Wyman impersonally. "If he's not a plant."

"I've used my ring. If you want to get it over with, we can test him and swear him in now."

They strapped him into a device that recorded pulse, perspiration, respiration, muscle tension and brainwaves. A sweatered specialist came and mildly asked Wyman matter-of-fact questions about his surroundings while he calibrated the polygraph.

Then came the payoff. Wyman did not fail to note that the sub commander loosened his gun in his holster when the question began.

"Name, age and origin?"

"Max Wyman. Twenty-two. Buffalo Syndic Territory."

"Do you like the Syndic?"

"I hate them."

"What are your feelings toward the North American Government?"

"If it's against the Syndic, I'm for it."

"Would you rob for the North American Government?"

"I would."

"Would you kill for it?"

"I would."

"Have you any reservations yet unstated in your answers?"

"No."

It went on for an hour. The questions were rephrased continuously; after each of Wyman's firm answers, the sweatered technician gave a satisfied little nod. At last it ended and he was unstrapped from the device.

The sub commander seemed a little awed as he got a small book and read from it: "**Do you,**

Max Wyman, solemnly renounce all allegiances previously held by you and pledge your allegiance to the North American Government?"

"I do," the young man said fiercely.

In a remote corner of his mind, for the first time in months, the bell ceased to ring, the pendulum to beat and the light to flash.

Charles Orsino knew again who he was and what was his mission.

SEVEN

It had begun when the girl led him through the conference room door. Naturally one had misgivings; naturally one didn't speak up. But the vaultlike door far downstairs was terrifying when it yawned before you and even more so when it closed behind you.

"What is this place?" he demanded at last. "Who are you?"

She said: "Psychology lab."

It had on him the same effect that "alchemy section" or "division of astrology" would have on a well-informed young man in 1980. He repeated flatly "Psychology lab. If you don't want to tell me, very well. I volunteered without strings." Which should remind her that he was a sort of hero and should be treated with a certain amount of dignity and that she could save her corny jokes.

"I meant it," she said, fiddling busily with the locks of yet another vaultlike door. "I'm a psychologist. I'm also, by the way, Lee Falcaro—since you asked."

"The old ma—Edward Falcaro's line?" he asked.

"Simon pure. He's my father's brother. Father's down in Miami, handling the tracks and gaming in general."

The second big door opened on a brain-gray room whose air had a curiously dead feel to it. "Sit down," she said, indicating a very unorthodox chair. He did, and found that the chair was the most comfortable piece of furniture he had ever known. Its contact with his body was so complete that it pressed nowhere, it poked nowhere. The girl studied dials in its back nevertheless and muttered something about adjusting it. He protested.

"Nonsense," she said decisively. She sat down herself in an ordinary seat. Charles shifted uneasily in his chair to find that it moved with him. Still no pressure, still no poking.

"You're wondering," she began, "about the word 'psychology.' It has a bad history and people have given it up as a bad job. It's true that there isn't pressure nowadays to study the human mind. People get along. In general what they want they get, without crippling effort. In your uncle Frank Taylor's language, the Syndic is an appropriately-structured organization of high morale and wide public acceptance. In my language, the Syndic is a father-image which does a good job of fathering. In good times, people aren't introspective.

"There is, literally, no reason why my line of the family should have kept up a tradition of experimental psychology. Way, way back, old Amadeo Falcaro often consulted Professor Oscar Sternweiss of the Columbia University psychology faculty—he wasn't as much of a dashing improviser as the history books make him out to be. Eventually one of his daughters married one of Sternweiss' sons and inherited the Sternweiss notebooks and library and apparatus. It became an irrational custom to keep it alive. When each academic school of psychology managed to prove that every other school of psychology was dead wrong and psychology collapsed as a science, the family tradition was unaffected; it stood outside the wrangling.

"Now, you're wondering what this has to do with trying to slip you into the Government."

"I am," Charles said fervently. If she'd been a doll outside the Syndic, he would minutes ago have protested that all this was foolish and walked out. Since she was not only in the Syndic, but in the Falcaro line, he had no choice except to hear her babble and *then* walk out. It was all rot, psychology. Id, oversoul, mind vectors, counseling, psychosomatics—rot from sick-minded old men. Everybody knew—

"The Government, we know, uses deinhibiting drugs as a first screening of its recruits. As an infallible second screening, they use a physiological lie-detector based on the fact that telling a lie causes tensions in the liar's body. We shall get around this by slipping you

in as a young man who hates the Syndic for
some valid reason—"

"Confound it, you were just telling me that
they can't be fooled!"

"We won't fool them. You'll *be* a young man
who hates the Syndic. We'll tear down your
present personality a gray cell at a time. We'll
pump you full of Seconal every day for half a
year . . . . We'll obliterate your personality
under a new one. We'll bury Charles Orsino
under a mountain of suggestions compul-
sions and obsessions shoveled at you sixteen hours a day while you're too groggy to
resist. Naturally the supplanting personality
will be neurotic, but that works in with the
mission."

He struggled with a metaphysical concept
for the first time in his life. "But—but—how
will I know I'm *me*?"

"We think we can put a trigger on it. When
you take the Government oath of allegiance,
you should bounce back."

He did not fail to note a little twin groove
between her brows that appeared when she
said *think* and *should*. He knew that in a sense
he was nearer death now than when Halloran's bullet had been intercepted.

"Are you staying with it?" she asked
simply.

Various factors entered into it. *A life for the
Syndic*, as in the children's history books.
That one didn't loom very large. But multiply
it by *it sounds like more fun than hot-rod polo*,
and that by *this is going to raise my stock sky-
high with the family* and you had something.

Somehow, under Lee Falcaro's interested gaze, he neglected to divide it by *if it works*.

"I'm staying with it," he said.

She grinned. "It won't be too hard," she said. "In the old days there would have been voting record, Social Security numbers, military service, addresses they could check on—hundreds of things. Now about all we have to fit you with is a name and a subjective life."

It began that spring day and went on into late fall.

The ringing bell.
The flashing light.
The wobbling pendulum.

You are Max Wyman of Buffalo Syndic Territory. You are Max Wyman of Buffalo Syndic Territory. You are Max Wyman of Buffalo Syndic . . .

Mom fried pork sausages in the morning, you loved the smell of pumpernickel from the bakery in Vesey Street.

Mr. Watsisname the English teacher with the mustache wanted you to go to college—

Nay, ye can not, though ye had Argus eyes,
In abbeyes they haue so many suttyll spyes;
For ones in the yere they have secret
    vvsytacyons,
And yf ony prynce reforme . . .

—but the stockyard job was closer, they needed breakdown men—

You are Max Wyman of Buffalo Syndic Territory. You are—

The ringing bell.
The flashing light.
The wobbling pendulum.
And the pork sausages and the teacher with
the mustache and poems you loved and

*page, 24, paragraph 3, maximum speed on a
live-cattle walkway is three miles per hour;
older walkways hold this speed with reduction
gears coupled to a standard 18-inch ehrenhafter unit. Standard practice in new con-
struction calls for holding speed by direct
drive from a specially wound ehrenhafter.
This places a special obligation in breakdown
maintenance men, who must distinguish between the two types, carry two sets of wiring
diagrams and a certain number of mutually
uninterchangeable parts, though good design
principles hold these to a minimum. The main
difference in the winding of a standard
18-incher and a low-speed ehrenhafter rotor—*

Of course things are better now, Max
Wyman, you owe a great debt to Jim Hogan,
Father of the Buffalo Syndic, who fought for
your freedom in the great old days, and to his
descendants who are tirelessly working for
your freedom and happiness.

And now happiness is a girl named Inge
Klohbel now that you're almost a man.

You are Max Wyman of Buffalo Syndic
Territory. You are Max Wyman of Buffalo
Syndic Territory

and Inge Klohbel is why you put away the
crazy dream of scholarship, for her lips and
hair and eyes and legs mean more to you than
anything, more than

Later phonologic changes include palatal mutation; i.e., before ht *and* hs *the diphthongs* eo, io, *which resulted from breaking, became* ie (i, y), *as in* cneoht, chieht, *and* ceox (x *equaling* hs), siex, six, syx . . .

the crazy dream of scholarship, what kind of a way is that to repay the Syndic and

The ringing bell.

The flashing light.

The wobbling pendulum.

repay the Syndic and young Mike Hogan all over the neighborhood suddenly and Inge says he did stop and say hello but of course he was just being polite

so you hit the manuals hard and one day you go out on a breakdown call and none of the older men could figure out why the pump was on the blink (a roaring, chewing monster of a pump it was, sitting there like a dead husk and the cattlefeed backed up four miles to a storage tank in the suburbs and the steers in the yards bawling with hunger) and you traced the dead wire, you out with the spotwelder, a zip of blue flame and the pump began to chew again and you got the afternoon off.

And there they were.

LEE FALCARO: (BENDING OVER THE MUTTERING, TWITCHING CARCASS) ADRENALIN. BRIGHTER PICTURE AND LOUDER SOUND. ASSISTANT: (OPENING A PINCH COCK IN THE TUBE THAT ENTERS THE ARM, INCREASING VIDEO CONTRAST, INCREASING AUDIO): HE'S WEAKENING.

LEE FALCARO: (IN A WHISPER) I KNOW. I KNOW. BUT THIS IS IT.

ASSISTANT: (INAUDIBLY) YOU COLD-BLOODED BITCH.

You are Max Wyman, you are Max Wyman, and you don't know what to do about the Syndic that betrayed you, about the girl who betrayed you with the living representative of the Syndic, about the dream of scholarship that lies in ruins, the love that lies in ruins after how many promises and vows, the faith of twenty years that lies in ruins after how many declarations.

The ringing bell.

The flashing light.

The wobbling pendulum.

And a double whisky with a beer chaser.

LEE FALCARO: THE ALCOHOL.

(IT DRIPS FROM A STERILE GRADUATE, TRICKLES THROUGH THE RUBBER TUBING AND INTO THE ARM OF THE MUMBLING, SWEATING CARCASS. THE MOLECULES MINGLE WITH THE MOLECULES OF SERUM: IN SECONDS THEY ARE WASHED AGAINST THE CELL-WALLS OF THE FOREBRAIN. THE CELL-WALLS, LATTICES OF JELLY, CRAWL AND RE-ARRANGE THEIR STRUCTURE AS THE ALCOHOL MOLECULES BUMBLE AGAINST THEM; THE LAT-TICES OF JELLY THAT WALL IN THE CYTOPLASM AND NUCLEAR JELLY BECOME THINNER THAN THEY WERE. STREAMS OF ELECTRONS THAT HAD COURSED IN FAMILIAR PATHS THROUGH CHAINS OF NEURONS FIND EASIER PATHS THROUGH THE POISON-THINNED CELL-WALLS. A "MEMORY" OR AN "IDEA" OR A "HOPE" OR A "VALUE" THAT WAS A CONFIGURATION OF NEURONS LINKED BY ELECTRON STREAMS VANISHES WHEN THE ELECTRON STREAMS FIND AN EASIER WAY TO

FLOW NEW "MEMORIES," "IDEAS," "HOPES"
AND "VALUES" THAT ARE CONFIGURATIONS OF
NEURONS LINKED BY ELECTRON STREAMS ARE
BORN.)

Love and loyalty die, but not as if they had
never been. Their ghosts remain, Max
Wyman, and you are haunted by them. They
hound you from Buffalo to Erie, but there is
no oblivion deep enough in the Mex joints, or
in Tampa tequila or Pittsburgh zubrovka or
New York gin.

You tell incurious people who came to the
place on the corner for a shot and some talk
that you're the best breakdown man that ever
came out of Erie; you tell them women are no
God-damn good, you tell them the Syndic—
here you get sly and look around with
drunken caution, lowering your voice—you
tell them the Syndic's no God-damned good,
and you drunkenly recite poetry until they
move away, puzzled and annoyed.

LEE FALCARO: (PASSING A WEARY HAND ACROSS
HER FOREHEAD) WELL, HE'S HAD IT. DISCONNECT
THE TUBES, GIVE HIM A 48-HOUR STRETCH IN BED
AND THEN GET HIM ON THE STREET POINTED TO-
WARDS RIVEREDGE.

ASSISTANT: DOES THE APPARATUS GO INTO DEAD
STORAGE?

LEE FALCARO: (GRIMACING UNCONTROLLABLY)
NO. UNFORTUNATELY, NO.

ASSISTANT: (INAUDIBLY, AS SHE PLUCKS NEEDLE-
TIPPED TUBES FROM THE CARCASS' ELBOWS)
WHO'S THE NEXT SUCKER?

EIGHT

The submarine surfaced at dawn. Orsino had been assigned a bunk and, to his surprise, had fallen asleep almost at once. At eight in the morning, he was shaken awake by one of the men in caps.

"Shift change," the man explained laconically.

Orsino started to say something polite and sleepy. The man grabbed his shoulder and rolled him onto the deck, snarling: "You going to *argue?*"

Orsino's reactions were geared to hot-rod polo—doing the split-second right thing after instinctively evaluating the roll of the ball, the ricochet of bullets, the probable tactics and strategy of the opposing four. They were not geared to a human being who behaved with the blind ferocity of an inanimate object. He just gawked at him from the deck, noting the man had one hand on a sheath knife.

"All right, buster," the man said contemptuously, apparently deciding that Orsino
would stay put. "Just don't mess with the
Guard." He rolled into the bunk and gave a
good imitation of a man asleep until Orsino
worked his way through the crowded compartment and up a ladder to the deck.

There was a heavy, gray overcast. The submarine seemed to be planing the water; salt
spray washed the shining deck. A gun crew
was forward, drilling with a five-inch launcher. The rasp of a petty officer singing out
the numbers mingled with the hiss and gurgle of the spray. Orsino leaned against the
conning tower and tried to comb his thoughts
out clean and straight.

It wasn't easy.

He was Charles Orsino, very junior Syndic
member, with all memories pertaining there-
to.

He was also, more dimly, Max Wyman, with
his memories. Now, able to stand outside of
Wyman, he could recall how those memories
had been implanted—down to the last stab of
the last needle. He thought some very bitter
thoughts about Lee Falcaro—and dropped
them, snapping to attention as Commander
Grinnel pulled himself through the hatch.
"Good morning, sir," he said.

The cold eyes drilled him. "Rest," the Commander said. "We don't play it that way on a
pigboat. I hear you had some trouble about
your bunk."

Orsino shrugged uncomfortably.

"Somebody should have told you," the Commander said. "The boat's full of Guardsmen. They have a very high opinion of themselves —which is correct. They carried off the raid in good style. You don't mess with Guards."

"What are they?" Orsino asked.

Grinnel shrugged. "The usual elite," he said. "Loman's gang." He noted Orsino's blank look and smiled coldly. "Loman's President of North America," he said.

"On shore," Orsino hazarded, "we used to hear about somebody named Ben Miller."

"Obsolete information. Miller had the Marines behind him. Loman was Secretary of Defense. He beached the Marines and broke them up into guard detachments. Took away their heavy weapons. Meanwhile, he built up the Guard, very quietly—which, with the Secretary of Information behind him, he could do. About two years ago, he struck. The Marines who didn't join the Guard were massacred. Miller had the sense to kill himself. The Veep and the Secretary of State resigned, but it didn't save their necks. Loman assumed the Presidency automatically, of course, and had them shot. They were corrupt as hell anyway. They were owned body and soul by the Southern Bloc."

Two seamen appeared with a folding cot, followed by the sub commander. He was red-eyed with lack of sleep. "Set it there," he told them, and sat heavily on the sagging canvas. "Morning, Grinnel," he said with an effort. "Believe I'm getting too old for the pigboats. I want sun and air. Think you can use your influence at court to get me a corvette?" He bared his teeth to show it was a joke.

Grinnel said, with a minimum smile: "If I had any influence, would I catch the cloak-and-dagger crap they sling at me?"

The sub commander swiveled his head ninety degrees port, ninety degrees starboard; faced about, and did the same thing to the rear. He saw nothing. He didn't expect to. There would be nothing in sight here unless it was a wandering ore boat from Mob territory, somewhere between the Great Lakes via St. Lawrence and the Gulf . . . but a sub commander did not pass the watch without taking that look. The captain rolled back onto the cot and was instantly asleep, a muscle twitching the left side of his face every few seconds.

Grinnel drew Orsino to the lee of the conning tower. "We'll let him sleep," he said. "Go tell that gun crew Commander Grinnel says they should lay below."

Orsino did. The petty officer said something exasperated about the gunnery training bill and Orsino repeated his piece. They secured the launcher and went below.

Grinnel said, with apparent irrelevance: "You're a rare bird, Wyman. You're capable —and you're uncommitted. Let's go below. Stick with me."

He followed the fat little Commander into the conning tower. Grinnel told an officer of some sort: "I'll take the con, mister. Wyman here will take the radar watch." He gave Orsino a look that choked off his protests. Presumably, Grinnel knew that he was ignorant of radar.

The officer, looking baffled, said: "Yes, Commander." A seaman pulled his head out of a facefitting box and told Wyman: "It's all yours, stranger." Wyman cautiously put his face into the box and was confronted by meaningless blobs of green, numerals in the dark, and a couple of arrows to make confusion complete.

He heard Grinnel say to the helmsman: "Get me a mug of joe, sailor. I'll take the wheel."

"I'll pass the word, sir."

"Nuts you'll pass the word, sailor. Go get the coffee—I want it now and not when some steward's mate decides he's ready to bring it."

"Aye, aye, sir." Orsino heard him clatter down the ladder. Then his arm was gripped and Grinnel's voice muttered in his ear: "When you hear me bitch about the coffee, sing out: 'Aircraft 265, DX 3,000.' Good and loud. No, don't stop looking. Repeat it."

Orsino said, his eyes crossing on double images of the meaningless, luminous blobs: "Aircraft 265, DX 3,000. Good and loud. When you bitch about the coffee."

"Right. Don't forget it."

He heard the feet on the ladder again. "Coffee, sir."

"Thanks, sailor." A long sip and then another. "I always said the pigboats drink the lousiest joe in the Navy."

"Aircraft 265, DX 3,000!" Orsino yelled.

A thunderous alarm began to sound. "Take her down!" yelled Commander Grinnel.

"Take her down, sir!" the helmsman echoed. "But sir, the skipper—"

Orsino remembered him too then, dead asleep in his cot on the deck, the muscle twitching the left side of his face every few seconds.

"God damn it, those were aircraft! *Take her down!*"

The luminous blobs and numbers and arrows swirled before Orsino's eyes as the trim of the ship changed, hatches clanged to and water thundered into the ballast tanks. He staggered and caught himself as the deck angled sharply underfoot.

He knew what Grinnel had meant by saying he was uncommitted, and he knew now that it was no longer true.

He thought for a moment that he might be sick into the face-fitting box, but it passed.

Minutes later, Grinnel was on the mike, his voice sounding metallically through the ship: "To all hands. To all hands. This is Commander Grinnel. We lost the skipper in that emergency dive—but you and I know that that's the way he would have wanted it. As senior line officer aboard, I'm assuming command for the rest of the voyage. We will remain submerged until dark. Division officers report to the wardroom. That's all."

He tapped Orsino on the shoulder. "Take off," he said. Orsino realized that the green blobs—clouds, were they?—no longer showed, and decided that air search radar didn't work through water.

He wasn't in on the wardroom meeting, and wandered rather forlornly through the ship, incredibly jammed as it was with sleeping men, coffee-drinking men and booty. Half a dozen times he had to turn away close questioning about his radar experience and the appearance of the aircraft on the radar scope. Each time he managed it, with the feeling that one more question would have cooked his goose.

The men weren't sentimental about the skipper they had lost. Mostly they wondered how much of a cut Grinnel would allot them from the booty of Cape Cod.

At last the word was passed for "Wyman" to report to the captain's cabin. He did, sweating after a fifteen-minute chat with a radar technician.

Grinnel closed the door of the minute cabin and smirked at him. "You have trouble, Wyman?" he asked.

"Yes."

"You'd have worse trouble if they found out for sure that you don't know radar. I'd be in the clear. I could tell them you claimed to be a qualified radar man. That would make me out to be pretty gullible, but it would make you out to be a murderer. Who's backing you, Wyman? Who told you to get rid of the skipper?"

"Quite right, sir," Orsino said. "You've really got me there."

"Glad you realize it, Wyman. I've got you and I can use you. It was a great bit of luck, the skipper corking off on deck. But I've always had a talent for improvisation. If you're determined to be a leader, Wyman, nothing is more valuable. Do you know, I can relax with you? It's a rare feeling. For once I can be certain that the man I'm talking to isn't one of Loman's stooges, or one of Clinch's NABI ferrets or anything else but what he says he is—

"But that's beside the point. I have something else to tell you. There are two sides to working for me, Wyman. One of them's punishment if you get off the track. That's been made clear to you. The other is reward if you stay on. I have plans, Wyman, that are large-scale. They simply eclipse the wildest hopes of Loman, Clinch, Baggot and the rest. And yet, they're not wild. How'd you like to be on the inside when the North American Government returns to the mainland?"

Orsino uttered an authentic gasp and Commander Grinnel looked satisfied.

NINE

The submarine docked at an indescribably
lovely bay in the South of Ireland. Orsino
asked Grinnel whether the Irish didn't object
to this, and was met with a blank stare. It
developed that the Irish consisted of a few
hundred wild men in the woods—maybe a few
thousand. The stupid shorebound personnel
couldn't seem to clean them out. Grinnel
didn't know anything about them, and he
cared less.

Ireland appeared to be the naval base. The
Government proper was located on Iceland,
vernal again after a long climatic swing. The
Canaries and Ascencion were outposts.

Orsino had learned enough on the voyage to
recognize the Government for what it was. It
had happened before in history; Uncle Frank
had pointed it out. Big-time Caribbean piracy
had grown from very respectable origins.
Gentlemen-skippers have been granted letters

of marque and reprisal by warring govern-
ments, which made them a sort of contract
navy. Periods of peace had found these
privateers unwilling to give up their hard-
learned complicated profession and their
investments in it. When they could no longer
hoist the flag of England or France or Spain,
they simply hoisted Jolly Roger and went it
alone.

Confusing? Quite! The famous Captain
Kidd thought he was a gallant privateer and
sailed trustingly into New York. Somewhere
he had failed to touch third base; they shipped
him to London for trial and hanged him as a
pirate. The famous Henry Morgan had never
been anything but a pirate and a super-pirate;
as admiral of a private fleet he executed a
brilliant amphibious operation and sacked
the city of Panama. He was knighted, made
governor of a fair-sized English island in the
West Indies and died loved and respected by
all.

Charles Orsino found himself a member of
a pirate band that called itself the North
American Government.

More difficult to learn were the ins and outs
of pirate politics, which were hampered with
an archaic, structurally inappropriate nomenclature and body of tradition. Commander
Grinnel was a Sociocrat, which meant that he
was in the same gang as President Loman. The
late sub commander had been a Constitutionist, which meant that he was allied with the
currently-out "Southern Bloc." The Southern
Bloc did not consist of Southerners at this

stage of the North American Government's history but of a clique that tended to include the engineers and maintenance men of the Government. That had been the reason for the sub commander's erasure. The Constitution-ists traditionally commanded pigboats and aircraft while surface vessels and the shore establishments were in the hands of the Socio-crats—the fruit of some long forgotten com-promise.

Commander Grinnel cheerfully explained to Charles that there was a crypto-Sociocrat naval officer primed and waiting to be ap-pointed to the command of the sub. The Constitutionist gang would back him to the hilt and the Sociocrats would growl and finally assent. If, thereafter, the Constitu-tionists ever counted on the sub in a coup, they would be quickly disillusioned.

There wasn't much voting. Forty years be-fore there had been a bad deadlock following the death by natural causes of President Powell after seventeen years in office. An ad hoc bipartisan conference called a session of the Senate and the Senate elected a new Presi-dent.

It was little information to be equipped with when you walked out into the brawling streets of New Portsmouth on shore leave.

The town had an improvised look which was strange to Orsino. There was a sanitation reactor every hundred yards or so, but he mis-trusted the look of the ground-level mains that led to it from the houses. There were house flies from which he shied violently.

Every other shack on the waterfront was a
bar or a notch joint. He sampled the goods at
one of the former and was shocked by the
quality and price. He rolled out, his ears still
ringing from the belt of raw booze, as half a
dozen sweatered Guards rolled in, singing
some esoteric song about their high morale. A
couple of them looked at him appraisingly, as
though they wondered what kind of a noise
he'd make if they jumped on his stomach real
hard, and he hurried away from them.

The other entertainment facilities of the
waterfront were flatly ruled out by a quick
inspection of the wares. He didn't know what
to make of them. Joints back in Syndic Territory, if you were a man, made sense. You went
to learn the ropes, or because you were afraid
of getting mixed up in something intense
when you didn't want to, or because you
wanted a change, or because you were too
busy, lazy or shy to chase skirts on your own.
If you were a woman and not too particular, a
couple of years in a joint left you with a considerable amount of money and some interesting memories which you were under no
obligation to discuss with your husbands or
husband.

But the sloppy beasts who called to him
from the windows of the joints here on the
waterfront left him puzzled and disgusted. He
reflected, strolling up Washington Street with
eyes straight ahead, that women must be in
short supply if they could make a living—or
that the male citizens of the Government had
no taste.

A whiff from one of those questionable sewer mains sent him reeling. He ducked into another saloon in self-defense and leaned groggily against the bar. A pretty brunette demanded: "What'll you have?"

"Gin, please." He peeled a ten off the roll Grinnel had given him. When the girl poured his gin he looked on her and found her fair. In all innocence, he asked her a question, as he might have asked a barmaid back home. She could have answered, "Yes," "No," "Maybe," or "What's in it for me?"

Instead she called him a lousy bastard, picked up a beer mug and was about to shatter it on his head when a hand caught her and a voice warned: "Hold it, Mabel! This guy's off my ship. He's just out of the States; he doesn't know any better. You know what it's like over there."

Mabel snarled: "You better wise him up then, friend. He can't go around talking like that to decent women." She slapped down another glass, poured gin and flounced down the bar.

Charles gulped his gin and turned shakily to his deliverer, a little reactor specialist he had seen on the sub once or twice. "Thanks," he said feeling inadequate. "Maybe you better wise me up. All I said was, 'Darling, do you—'"

The reactor man held up his hand. "That's enough," he said. "You don't talk that way over here unless you want your scalp parted."

Charles, buzzing a little with the gin, protested hotly: "But what's the harm? All she had to say was no; I wasn't going to throw her down on the floor!"

A shrug. "I heard about things in the States —Wyman, isn't it? I guess I didn't really believe it. You mean I could go up to any woman and just ask her how's about it?"

"Within reason, yes."

"And *do* they?"

"Some do, some don't—like here."

"Like hell, like here! Last liberty—" and the reactor man told him a long, confusing story about his adventures and his difficulties with the "decent" women of the Government.

Charles left the saloon fully conscious that values were different here. He was beginning to understand the sloppy beasts in the windows of the notch joint and why men could bring themselves to settle for nothing better. He was also overwhelmed by a great wave of homesickness.

The ugly pattern was beginning to emerge. Prudery, rape, frigidity, intrigue for power— and assassination? Beyond the one hint, Grinnel had said nothing that affected Syndic Territory.

But nothing would be more logical than for this band of brigands to lust after the riches of the continent.

Back of the waterfront were shipfitting shops and living quarters. Work was being done by a puzzling combination of mechanization and musclepower. In one open shed he saw a lathe-hand turning a gun barrel out of a forging; the lathe was driven by one of those standard 18-inch ehrenhaft rotors Max

Wyman knew so well. But a vertical drill press next to it—Orsino blinked. Two men, sweating and panting, were turning a stubborn vertical drum as tall as they were, and a belt drive from the drum whirled the drill bit as it sank into a hunk of bronze. The men were in rags, dirty rags. And it came to Orsino with a stunning shock when he realized what the dull, clanking things were that swung from their wrists. The men were chained to the handles of the wheel.

He walked on, almost dazed, comprehending now some cryptic remarks that had been passed aboard the sub.

"No Frog has staying power. Give a Limey his beef once a day and he'll outsweat a Frog."

"Yeah, but you can't whip a Limey. They just go bad when you whip a Limey."

"They just get sullen for a while. But let me tell you, friend, don't ever whip a Spig. You whip a Spig, he'll wait twenty years if he has to but he'll *get* you, right between the ribs."

"If a Spig wants to be boiled, I should worry."

It had been broken up in laughter.

Boiled! Could such things be?

Sixteen ragged, filth-crusted sub-humans were creeping down the road, each straining at a rope. An inch at a time, they were dragging a skid loaded with one huge turbine gear whose tiny herringbone teeth caught the afternoon sun.

The Government had reactors, the Government had vehicles—why this? He slowly realized that the Government's metal and machinery and atomic power went into its warships; that there was none left over for consumers and the uses of peace. The Government had degenerated into a dawn-age monster, specialized all to teeth and claws and muscles to drive them with. The Government was now, whatever it had been, a graceless, humorless incarnate ferocity. Whatever lightness or joy survived was the meaningless vestigial twitching of an obsolete organ.

Somewhere a child began to bawl and Charles was surprised to feel a profound pity welling up in him. Like a sedentary man who after a workout aches in muscles he never knew he owned, Charles was discovering that he had emotions which had never been poignantly evoked by the bland passage of the hours in Syndic Territory.

Poor little kid, he thought, growing up in this hellhole. I don't know what having slaves to kick around will do to you, but I don't see how you can grow up a human being. I don't know what fear of love will do to you—make you a cheat? Or a graceless rutting animal with a choice only between graceless rutting violence and a stinking scuffle with a flabby and abstracted stranger in a strange unloved room? We have our guns to play with and they're good toys, but I don't know what kind of monster you'll become when they give you a gun to live with and violence for a god.

Reiner was right, he thought unhappily. *We've got to do something about this mess.*

A man and a woman were struggling in an alley as he passed. Old habit almost made him walk on, but this wasn't the playful business of ripping clothes as practiced during hilarious moments in Syndic Territory. It was a grim and silent struggle—

The man wore the sweater of the Guards. Nevertheless, Charles walked into the alley and tore him away from the woman; or rather, he yanked at the man's rocklike arm and the man, in surprise, let go of the woman and spun to face him.

"Beat it," Charles said to the woman, not looking around. He saw from the corner of his eye that she was staying right there.

The man's hand was on his sheath knife. He told Charles: "Get lost. Now. You don't mess with the Guards."

Charles felt his knees quivering, which was good. He knew from many a chukker of polo that it meant that he was strung to the breaking point, ready to explode into action. "Pull that knife," he said, "and the next thing you know you'll be eating it."

The man's face went dead calm and he pulled the knife and came in low, very fast. The knife was supposed to catch Charles in the middle. If Charles stepped inside it, the man would grab him in a bear hug and knife him in the back.

He caught the thick wrist from above with his left hand as the knife flashed toward his middle, and shoved out. He felt the point catch and slice his cuff. The Guardsman tried a furious and ill-advised kick at his crotch; with his grip on the knife-hand, Charles toppled him into the filthy alley as he stood one-legged and off-balance. He fell on his back, floundering, and for a black moment, Charles thought his weight was about to tear the wrist loose from his grip. The moment passed, and Charles put his right foot in the socket of the Guardsman's elbow, reinforced his tiring left hand with his right and leaned, doubling the man's forearm over the fulcrum of his boot. The man roared and dropped the knife. It had taken perhaps five seconds.

Charles said, panting: "I don't want to break your arm or kick your head in or anything like that. I just want you to go away and leave the woman alone." He was conscious of her, vaguely hovering in the background. He thought angrily: *She might at least get his knife.*

The Guardsman said thickly: "You give me the boot and I swear to God I'll find you and cut you to ribbons if it takes me the rest of my life."

Good, Charles thought. *Now he can tell himself he scared me. Good.* He let go of the forearm, straightened and took his foot from the man's elbow, stepping back. The Guardsman got up stiffly, flexing his arm, and stooped to pick up and sheath the knife. He spat in the dust at Charles' feet. "Yellow bastard," he said. "If the goddamn crow was worth it, I'd cut your heart out." He walked off down the alley and Charles followed him with his eyes until he turned the corner into the street.

Then he turned, irritated that the woman had not spoken.

She was Lee Falcaro.

"Lee!" he said, thunderstruck. "What are you doing here?" It was the same face, feature for feature, and between her brows appeared the same double groove he had seen before. But she didn't know him.

"You know me?" she asked blankly. "Is that why you pulled that ape off me? I ought to thank you. But I can't place you at all. I don't know many people here. I've been ill, you know."

There was a difference apparent now. The voice was a little querulous. And Charles would have staked his life that never could Lee Falcaro have said in that slightly smug, slightly proprietary, slightly aren't-I-interesting tone: "I've been ill, you know."

"But what are you *doing* here? Damn it, don't you know me? I'm Charles Orsino!"

He realized then that he had made a horrible mistake.

"Orsino," she said. And then she spat: *"Orsino! of the Syndic!"* There was black hatred in her eyes.

She turned and raced down the alley. He stood there stupidly, for almost a minute, and then ran after her, as far as the alley's mouth. She was gone. You could run almost anywhere in New Portsmouth in almost a minute.

A weedy little seaman wearing crossed quills on his cap was lounging against a building. He snickered at Charles. "Don't chase that one, sailor," he said. "She is the property of ONI."

"You know who she is?"

The yeoman happily spilled his inside dope

to the fleet gob: "Lee Bennet. Smuggled over here couple months ago by D.A.R. The hottest thing that ever hit Naval Intelligence. Very small potato in the Syndic—knows all the families, who does what, who's a figurehead and who's a worker. Terrific! Inside stuff! Hates the Syndic. A gang of big-timers did her dirt."

"Thanks," Charles said, and wandered off down the street.

It wasn't surprising. He should have *expected* it.

Noblesse oblige.

Pride of the Falcaro line. She wouldn't send anybody into deadly peril unless she were ready to go herself.

Only somehow the trigger that would have snapped neurotic, synthetic Lee Bennet into Lee Falcaro hadn't worked.

He wandered on aimlessly, wondering whether it would be minutes or hours before he'd be picked up and executed as a spy.

TEN

It took minutes only.

He had headed back to the waterfront, afraid to run, with some vague notion of stealing a boat or seeking the protection of Commander Grinnel. Before he reached the row of saloons and joints, a smart-looking squad of eight tall men overtook him.

"Hold it, mister," a sergeant said. He halted and the sergeant studied him. "Are you Orsino?"

"No," he said hopelessly. "That crazy woman began to yell at me that I was Orsino, but I'm not. My name's Wyman. What's this about, sergeant?"

The other men fell in beside and behind him. "We're stepping over to ONI," the sergeant said. "Do you walk or do we carry you?"

"There's the son of a bitch!" somebody bawled. Suddenly there were a dozen sweat-

ered Guardsmen around them. Their leader
was the thug Orsino had beaten in a fair fight.
He said silkily to the sergeant: "We want that
boy, leatherneck. Tell your squad to blow."

The sergeant went pale. "He's wanted for
questioning by the ONI," he said. "He's a
Syndic spy. Have you got orders?"

There was a drunken laugh. "Get the
Marine three-striper!" the Guardsman chor-
tled. "Orders!" He stuck his jaw into the
sergeant's face. "We don't need orders for
what we're going to do to him, leatherneck.
Tell your squad to blow. You Marines ought
to know by now that you don't mess with the
Guard."

A very junior officer appeared. "What's
going on here, you men?" he shrilled. "Atten-
shun!" He was ignored as Guardsman and
Marines measured one another with their
eyes, tensely. "I said *attention!* Dammit, Sergeant, *report!*" There was no reaction. The
officer yelled: "You men may think you can
get away with this but by God, you're wrong!"
He strode away, his fists clenched and his
face very red.

Orsino saw him stride through a gate into a
lot marked "Bupers Motor Pool." And he felt
a sudden wave of communal understanding
that there were only seconds to go before they
were interfered with. The Marine sergeant
played for time: "I'll be glad to surrender the
prisoner," he started, "if you have anything to
show in the way of—"

The Guardsman kicked for the pit of the
sergeant's stomach. He was a sucker, Orsino

thought abstractedly as he saw the sergeant
catch his foot, dump him in the road and pivot
to block another Guardsman. Then he was
fighting for his life himself, against three
bellowing Guardsmen.

A ripping, hammering noise filled the air
suddenly. Like cold magic, it froze the milling
mob where it stood. Fifty-caliber noise.

The jaygee was back, this time in a jeep with
a twin-fifty mounted over the hood. And he
was glaring down its barrels into the thick of
the crowd. People were beginning to stream
from the saloons, joints and shipfitting shops,
ringing the grim scene in.

The jaygee took one hand from the vibra-
ting gunmount to cock his cap rakishly over
one eye. *"Fall in!"* he rasped, and a haunting
air of familiarity came over Orsino. It was
quite three seconds before he placed it—
three seconds during which Marines and
Guardsmen were sorting themselves into
squads.

The waiting jeep, almost bucking in its
eagerness to be let loose—Orsino on the
ground, knees trembling with tension—it was
a perfect change of mount scene in a polo
match. He reacted automatically, breaking
for the jeep.

There was a surrealist flash of the jaygee's
face, suddenly flustered and dismayed, before
he clipped his tail over tea-kettle into the back
of the square little truck. There was another
flash of spectators scrambling left and right
as he roared the jeep down the road.

From then on, it was just a question of

hanging on to the wheel with one hand, trying to secure the free-traversing twin-fifty with the other, glancing back to see if the jaygee was still out, avoiding yapping dogs and pedestrians, staying on the rutted road, pushing all the possible speed out of the jeep, noting landmarks, and estimating the possibility of dangerous pursuit. For a two-goal polo player, a dull little practice session.

The road, such as it was, wound five miles inland through scrubby, second-growth woodland and terminated at a lumber camp where chained men in rags were dragging logs to a chuffing steam sawmill. When Orsino saw the shine of weapons on the men who weren't working, he spun the jeep 180 degrees, backtracked a quarter-mile and took off overland in a kidney-cracking hare and hounds course at fifty miles an hour. He didn't bother swerving for timber less than two inches in diameter.

The jeep took it for an hour in the fading afternoon light and then bucked to a halt. Orsino turned for an overdue check on the jaygee and found him conscious, but greenly clinging to the sides of the vehicle. "Christ," he was mumbling. "Oh, Christ." But he saw Orsino staring, and gamely struggled to his feet, standing in the truck bed. "You're under arrest, sailor," he said. "Striking an officer, abuse of government property, driving a government vehicle without a trip-ticket—" his legs betrayed him and he sat down, hard.

Orsino thought very briefly of tying him up, of letting him have a burst from the twin-fifty, of hitting him over the head with a wrench, and abandoned each idea.

He seemed to have loused up everything so far, but he was still on a mission. For the first time he had a commissioned officer of the Government approximately in his power, if only until his landlegs returned. He snapped: "Nonsense. *You're* under arrest."

The jaygee seemed to be reviewing rapidly any transgressions he may have committed, and asked at last, cautiously: "By what authority?"

"I represent the Syndic."

It was a blockbuster. The jaygee stammered: "But you can't—but there isn't any way—but how—"

"Never mind how."

"You're crazy. You must be, or you wouldn't stop here. I don't believe you're from the Continent and I don't believe the jeep's broken down." He was beginning to sound just a little hysterical. "It can't break down here. We must be more than thirty miles inland."

"What's special about thirty miles inland?"

"The natives, you fool!"

The natives again. "I'm not worried about natives. Not with a pair of fifties."

"You don't understand," the jaygee said, forcing calm into his voice. "This is the Outback. They're in charge here. We can't do a thing with them out. They jump people in the dark and skewer them. Now fix this damn jeep and let's get rolling!"

"Into a firing squad? Don't be silly, Lieutenant. I presume you won't slug me while I check the engine?"

The jaygee was looking around him. "My God, no," he said. "You may be a gangster, but—" He trailed off.

Orsino stiffened. Gangster was semi-dirty talk. "Listen, pirate," he said nastily, "I don't believe—"

"Pirate?" the jaygee roared indignantly, and then shut his mouth with a click, looking apprehensively about. The gesture wasn't faked; it alarmed Orsino.

"Tell me about your wildmen," he said.

"Go to hell," the jaygee said sulkily.

"Look, you called me a gangster first. What about these natives? You were trying to trick me, weren't you?"

"Kiss my royal North American eyeball, gangster."

"Don't be childish," Charles reproved him, feeling adult and superior. (The jaygee seemed to be a couple of years younger than he.) He climbed out of the seat and lifted the hood. The damage was trivial; a shear pin in the transmission had given way when he tried to bowl over a six-inch tree. He reported mournfully: "Cracked block. The jeep's through forever. You can get on your way, Lieutenant. I won't try to hold you."

The jaygee fumed: "You couldn't hold me if you wanted to, gangster. If you think I'm going to try and hoof back to the base alone in the dark, you're crazy. We're sticking together. Two of us may be able to hold them off for the night. In the morning, we'll see."

Well, maybe the officer did *believe* there were wildmen in the woods. That didn't mean there *were*.

The jaygee got out and looked under the hood uncertainly. It was obvious that in the first place he was no mechanic and in the second place he couldn't conceive of anybody voluntarily risking the woods rather than the naval base. "Uh-huh," he said. "Cracked all to hell. Dismount that gun while I get a fire started."

"Yes, sir," Charles said sardonically, saluting. The jaygee absently returned the salute and began to collect twigs.

He had the left unit off the mount when the jaygee slipped up to him in the gathering dusk and whispered: "Quiet! Switch on the headlights!"

Charles did, muttering: "What's this all about?"

"Quiet! I think I saw a deer. If the wind's right, he won't scent the machine. Get on that other barrel."

The headlights bored twin tunnels of brightness through the woods and then, startlingly, a graceful animal head appeared, blinking, twenty yards away. "Give him a burst," the jaygee whispered.

Charles smoothly and quietly went through the drill: open the receiver, clear it, close it, half-load, insert the link, full load, lift the sight, set the sight, set the screw for sticky traverse, set the elevation, get the sight picture, lower the sight—

The damndest thing happened then. All

ready to tap the triggers delicately, he noticed
that the muzzle of the gun was weaving and
hitching around the head of the dazzled deer.
And furthermore, that his unorthodox and incorrect death grip on the handle of the gun
was causing it to weave and hitch. It was not
as bad as it would have been if he'd been
stuffed full of dire warnings about buck fever,
but it was pretty bad.

"Go on! Go on!" whispered the jaygee
angrily.

He closed his eyes, gritted his teeth and
yanked. A thunderous twenty-round burst
was on its way before he could unclamp his
fingers.

"You got him, all right," the jaygee said
doubtfully. "Take that loose barrel and let's
go see."

Sweating unaccountably, Charles counted
out twenty rounds from the end of a belt and
pulled out cartridge number twenty-one. He
loaded the twenty-round strip into the loose
gun and hefted it. Nuts, he decided, and pulled
out cartridge number seven, letting eight
through twenty crash to the ground. Staggering, he followed the jaygee down the bright
twin tunnel of light and found him standing
over a tatter of flesh.

"Man," the officer said, "what an A-1
screwup you are! First you wreck the jeep.
Then you hit a fifty-pound deer with eighty
pounds of ammo. It isn't even hamburger!"

"So why didn't you shoot?" he demanded.

"I should have," the jaygee said bitterly. "I
don't happen to be checked out on the fifty

and I thought you'd do a better job of pot-hunting." He picked up a gobbet of meat that sparkled with fragments of soft-nosed bullets, studied it and dropped it again. "Let's get back to the jeep."

They trudged back. Orsino asked: "How do these aborigines of yours operate?"

"Sneak up in the dark. They have spears and a few stolen guns. Usually they don't have cartridges for them but you can't count on that. But they have . . . witches."

Orsino snorted. He was getting very hungry indeed. "Do you know any of the local plants we might eat?"

The jaygee said confidently: "I guess we can get by on roots until morning."

Orsino leaned the fifty against the jeep. He dubiously pulled up a shrub, dabbed clods off its root and tasted it. It tasted exactly like a root. He sighed and changed the subject. "What do we do with the fifties when I get them both off the mount?"

"The jeep mount breaks down some damn way or other into two low-mount tripods. See if you can figure it out while I get the fire going."

The jaygee had a very small, very smokey fire barely going in twenty minutes. Orsino was still struggling with the jeep gun mount. It came apart, but it wouldn't go together again. The jaygee strolled over at last contemptuously to lend a hand. He couldn't make it work either.

"Look," Orsino said, exasperated. "We're okay on the azimuth circle, we're okay on the elevating screw, we're okay on the rear leg—I think. There must be *some* way the two front legs hook on!''

Two lost tempers and four split fingernails later it developed that the "elevating screw" really held the two front legs on and that you elevated by adjusting the rear tripod leg. ''A hell of an officer you are,'' Orsino sulked.

It began to rain then, putting the small smoky fire out with a hiss. They wound up prone under the jeep, not on speaking terms, each tending a gun, each presumably responsible for 180 degrees of perimeter.

Charles was fairly dry, except for a trickle of icy water following a contour that meandered to his left knee. After an hour of eye-straining—nothing to be seen—and ear-straining—only the patter of rain—he heard a snore and kicked the jaygee.

The jaygee cursed wearily and said: ''I guess we'd better talk to keep awake.''

''*I'm* not having any trouble, pirate.''

''Oh, knock it off—where do you get that pirate bit, gangster?''

''You're outlaws, aren't you?''

''Like hell we are. *You're* the outlaws. You rebelled against the lawfully constituted North American Government. Just because you won—for the time being—doesn't mean you were right.''

''The fact that we won does mean that we were right. The fact that your so-called Government lives by raiding and scavenging off us means you were wrong. God, the things I've seen since I joined up with you thugs!''

"I'll bet. Respect for the home, sanctity of marriage, sexual morality, law and order —you never saw anything like that back home, did you gangster?"

Orsino clenched his teeth. "Somebody's been telling you a pack of lies," he said. "There's just as much home and family life and morality and order back in Syndic Territory as there is here. And probably a lot more."

"Bull. I've seen intelligence reports; I know how you people live. Are you telling me you don't have sexual promiscuity? Polygamy? Polyandry? Open gambling? Uncontrolled liquor trade? Corruption and shakedowns?"

Orsino squinted along the barrel of the gun into the rain. There was just truth enough in that for it to be tricky. "Look," he said, "take me as an average young man from Syndic Territory. I know maybe a hundred people— that's just a guess. I know just three women and two men who are what you'd call promiscuous. I know one family with two wives and one husband. Since we're talking, I'll mention one you missed—a mixed foursome I used to know, but they've broken up into two couples since. I don't really know any people personally who go in for polyandry, but I've met three casually. And the rest are ordinary middle-aged couples."

"Ah-*hah!* Middle-aged! Do you mean to tell me you're just leaving out anybody under middle age when you talk about morality?"

"Naturally," Charles said, baffled. "Wouldn't you?"

The only answer was a snort.

"What are bupers?" Charles asked.

"Bu-Pers," the jaygee said distinctly. "Bureau of Personnel, North American Navy."

"What do you do there?"

"What would a personnel bureau do?" the jaygee said patiently. "We recruit, classify, assign, promote and train personnel."

"Paperwork, huh? No wonder you don't know how to shoot or drive."

"If I didn't need you to cover my back, I'd shove this MG down your silly throat. For your information, gangster, all officers do a tour of duty on paperwork before they're assigned to their permanent branch. I'm going into the pigboats."

"Why?"

"Family. My father commands a sub. He's Captain Van Dellen."

Oh, God. Van Dellen. The sub commander Grinnel—and he—had murdered. The kid hadn't heard yet that his father had been "lost" in an emergency dive.

The rain ceased to fall; the pattering drizzle gave way to irregular, splashing drops from leaves and branches.

"Van Dellen," Charles said. "There's something you ought to know."

"It'll keep," the jaygee answered in a grim whisper. The bolt of his gun clicked from half-load to full. "I hear them out there."

ELEVEN

She felt the power of the goddess working in her, but feebly. Dark ... so dark ... and so tired ... how old was she? More than eight hundred moons had waxed and waned above her head since birth. And she had run at the head of her spearmen when they heard the guns to the sound of the guns. Guns meant the smithymen from the sea, and you killed smithymen when you could.

She let out a short shrill chuckle in the dark. There was a rustling of branches. One of the spearmen had turned to stare at the sound. She knew his face was worried. "Tend to business, you fool!" she wheezed. "Or by Bridget—" His breath went in with a hiss and she chuckled again. You had to let them know who was the cook and who was the potatoes every now and then. Kill the fool? Not now; not when there were smithymen with guns waiting to be taken.

The power of the goddess worked stronger in her withered breast as her rage grew at their impudence. Coming into *her* woods with their stinking metal! She would gut them well.

There were two of them. A toothless grin slit her old face. She had not taken two smithymen together for thirty moons. For all her wrinkles and creaks, what a fine vessel she was for the power, to be sure! Her worthless, slow-to-learn niece could run and jump and she had a certain air, but she'd never be such a vessel. Her sister—the crone spat— these were degenerate days. In the old days, her sister would have been spitted when she refused the ordeal in her youth. The little one now, whatever her name was, she would make a *fine* vessel for the power when she was gathered to the goddess. If her sister or her niece didn't hold her head under water too long, or have a spear shoved too deep into her gut or hit her on the head with too heavy a rock.

These were degenerate days. She had poisoned her own mother to become the vessel of power, and that was right because a true vessel of power vomits up poison before it can kill.

The spearmen to her right and left shifted uneasily. She heard a faint mumble of the two smithymen talking. Let them talk! Doubtless they were cursing the goddess obscenely; doubtless that was what the smithymen all did when their mouths were not stuffed with food.

She thought of the man called Kennedy who forged spearheads and arrowpoints for her people—he was a strange one, touched by the goddess, which proved her infinite power. She could touch and turn the head of even a smithyman. He was a strange one. Well now, to get on with it. She wished the power were working stronger in her; she was tired and could hardly see. But by the grace of the goddess there would be two new heads over her holy hut come dawn. She could hardly see, but the goddess wouldn't fail her . . . .

She quavered like a screech-owl, and the spearmen began to slip forward through the brush. She was not allowed to eat honey lest its sweetness clash with the power in her, but the taste of power was sweeter than the taste of honey.

It was no louder than the big, splashing drops from the trees but different in kind: the rustling passage of big bodies, clumsier than animals', and the mutter of voices.

With frightful suddenness there was an ear-splitting shriek and a trampling rush of feet. By sheer reflex, Orsino clamped down on the trigger of his fifty, and his brain rocked at its world-filling thunder. Shadowy figures were blotted out by the orange muzzle-flash. You're supposed to fire neat, spaced bursts of eight, he told himself. You're supposed to set the screw on the azimuth ring for a sticky, draggy feel and traverse the gun by clipping it neatly with the heel of your palm. I wonder what old Gilby would say if he could see his star pupil burning out a barrel and swinging his gun like a fire hose? "Confound you, Charles"—he remembered the old pro's weatherbeaten croak —"did you come out today to disgrace yourself and waste my time?"

The gun stopped firing; end of the belt. Twenty, fifty or a hundred rounds? He didn't remember. He clawed for another belt and smoothly, in the dark, loaded again and listened.

"You all right, gangster?" the jaygee said behind him, making him jump.

"Yes," he said. "Will they come back?"

"I don't know."

"You bitches' bastards," an agonized voice wheezed from the darkness. "Me back is broke, you bitches' bastards." And the voice began to sob.

They listened to it in silence for perhaps a minute. It seemed to come from Orsino's left front. At last he said to the jaygee: "If the rest are gone maybe we can do something for him. At least make him comfortable."

"Too risky," the jaygee said after a long pause.

The sobbing went on, and as the excitement of the attack drained from Orsino, he felt deathly tired, cramped and thirsty. The thirst he could do something about. He scooped water from the muddy runnel by his knee and sucked it from his palms twice. The third time, he thought of the thirst that the sobbing creature out in the dark must be feeling, and his hand wouldn't go to his mouth.

"I'm going to get him," he whispered to the jaygee.

"Stay where you are! That's an order!"

He didn't answer, but began to work his cramped and aching body from under the jeep. The jaygee, a couple of years younger and lither than he, slid out first from his own side. Orsino sighed and relaxed as he heard his footsteps cautiously circle the jeep.

"Finish me off!" the wounded man was sobbing. "For the love of the goddess, finish me off, you bitches' bastards! You've broke me back—*ah!*" That was a cry of savage delight.

There was a strangled noise from the jaygee and then only a soft, deadly thrashing noise from the dark. Hell, Orsino thought bitterly. And it was my idea. He snaked out from under the jeep and raced through wet brush.

The two of them were a tangled knot of darkness rolling on the ground. A naked back came uppermost; Orsino fell on it and clawed at its head. He felt a huge beard, took two handfuls of it and pulled as hard as he could. There was a wild screech and a flailing of arms. The jaygee broke away and stood up, panting hoarsely. Charles heard a sharp crunch and a snap, and the flailing sweaty figure beneath him lay still.

"Back to the guns," the jaygee choked. He swayed, and Orsino took him by the arm. On the way back to the jeep, they stumbled over something that was certainly a body.

Orsino's flesh shrank from lying down again in the muddy hollow behind his gun, but he did, shivering. He heard the jaygee thud wearily into position. "What did you do to him?" he asked. "Is he dead?"

"Kicked him," the jaygee choked. "I guess

so. His head snapped back and there was that crack. I guess he's dead. I never heard of that broken-wing trick from them before. I guess he just wanted to take one more with him. They have a kind of religion."

The jaygee sounded as though he was teetering on the edge of a breakdown. Make him mad, intuition said to Orsino. He might go howling off among the trees unless he snaps out of it.

"It's a hell of a way to run an island," he said nastily. "You buggers were chased out of North America because you couldn't run things right and now you can't even control a lousy little island more than five miles inland." He added with deliberate, superior amusement: "Of course, they've got witches."

"Shut your mouth, gangster—*I'm warning you.*" The note of hysteria was still there. And then the jaygee said dully: "I didn't mean that. I'm sorry. You did come out and help me after all."

"Surprised?"

"Yes. Twice. First time when you wanted to go out yourself. I suppose you can't help being born where you were. Maybe if you came over to us all the way, the Government would forgive and forget. But no—I suppose not." He paused, obviously casting about for a change of subject. He still seemed sublimely confident that they'd get back to the naval base with him in charge of the detail. "What ship did you cross in?"

"Atom sub *Taft*," Orsino said. He could have bitten his tongue out when he realized what he'd let slip.

"Taft? That's my father's pigboat! Captain Van Dellen. How is he? I was going down to the dock when—when the rhubarb started."

"He's dead," Orsino said flatly. "He was caught on deck during an emergency dive."

The jaygee said nothing for a while and then uttered an unconvincing low laugh of disbelief. "You're lying," he said. "His crew'd never let that happen. They worship him. They'd let the ship be blown to hell before they took her down without the skipper."

"Commander Grinnel had the con. He ordered the dive and roared down the crew when they wanted to get your father inboard. I'm sorry."

"Grinnel," the jaygee whispered. "Grinnel. Yes, I know Commander Grinnel. He's—he's a good officer. He must have done it because he had to. Tell me about it, please."

It was more than Orsino could bear. "Your father was murdered," he said harshly. "I know because Grinnel put me on radar watch —and I don't know a God-damned thing about reading a radarscope. He told me to sing out 'enemy planes' and I did because I didn't know what the hell was going on. He used that as an excuse to crash-dive while your father was sleeping on deck. His cheek was twitching while he slept, he was so tired. And your good officer murdered him."

He heard the jaygee sobbing hoarsely. At last he asked Orsino in a dry, choked voice: "Politics?"

"Politics," Orsino said. "Grinnel evidently expected to use me as his high-class private assassin, so he told me the score. He killed your father so a secret Sociocrat would get his pigboat command—somebody who's been posing as a Constitutionist but really is a Sociocrat."

"Ah," the jaygee said softly. "Commander Folkstone. Exec on Kindler's *Constitution*. A Sociocrat, is he? Grinnel and Folkstone, eh?"

Orsino jumped wildly as the jaygee's machine gun began to roar a long burst of twenty, but he didn't fire himself. As if he could read the jaygee's mind, he knew that there was no enemy out there in the dark, and that the bullets were aimed only at two absent phantoms. He said nothing.

"We've got to get to Iceland," the jaygee said at last, soberly.

"Iceland?"

"This is one for the CC of the Constitutionists. The Central Committe. It's a breach of the Freiberg Compromise. It means we call the Sociocrats, and if they don't make full restitution—war."

"I don't know what you're talking about, Van Dellen. And what do you mean, *we?*"

"You and I. You're the source of the story; you're the one who'd be lie-tested."

"Mister, if they lie-tested me, I'd be shot down in the chair!"

"Not with the Constitutionist CC protecting you," the jaygee said sharply, as if offended. "Damn it, man, why are you hesitating? Aren't you a Constitutionist?"

"My God, no! How can I be anything like that when I've just got into your—into the Government?"

"But don't you believe in the general principles of Constitutionism?"

Orsino asked guardedly: "What are they?"

"Dignity of the individual. Government of laws and not of men. Respect for the family. Loyalty to the party organization."

Orsino thought it over carefully. Dignity of the individual? No; he doubted that he believed in it. Individuals were pretty funny and always making mistakes. Back home you got along much better if you didn't go in for such a haughty austere notion and took it for granted that there'd be a lot of bungling by you and everybody you ran into.

Government of laws and not of men? Not in Syndic Territory! It was a government of men there, and a pretty good one. Uncle Frank said it would continue to be a good government only as long as its morale was maintained and it kept the credit of the governed. Until things got a lot worse in Syndic Territory it would be insane to switch from government of men to a government of laws. And when they did, it would be insane not to.

Respect for the family? Oh, sure. As long as the family was respectable, he'd respect it.

Loyalty to the party organization? Depended entirely on the party organization. No doubt the Constitutionists were stinking murderers just like the Sociocrats.

"I suppose," he said slowly, "I'm a Constitutionist at heart, Van Dellen. After all, some things are universal."

The jaygee said: "I hoped you'd say that. The way you left the gun to help me—I was sure then that you've been misguided, but that you're fundamentally sound."

You've got him, Orsino told himself, but don't be fool enough to count on it. He's been lightheaded from hunger and no sleep and the shock of his father's death. You helped him in a death struggle and there's team spirit working on him. The guy covering my back, how can I fail to trust him, how could I dare not to trust him? But don't be fool enough to count on it after he's slept. Meanwhile, push it for all it's worth.

"What are your plans?" he asked gravely.

"We've got to slip out of Ireland by sub or plane," the jaygee brooded. "We can't go to the New Portsmouth or ComSurf organizations; they're Sociocrat. My God! Maybe even ComSub and ComAv are rotten if Folkstone's been reached! Grinnel will have passed the word to the Sociocrats that you're out of control."

"What does that mean?"

"Death," the jaygee said.

TWELVE

Commander Grinnel, after reporting formally, had gone straight to a joint. It wasn't until midnight that he got The Word, from a friendly ONI lieutenant who had dropped into the house.

"What?" Grinnel roared. "Who is this woman? Where is she? Take me to her at once!"

"Commander!" the lieutenant said aghast, "I just got here."

"You heard me, mister! At once!"

The unhappy lieutenant made his apologies while Grinnel dressed. On their way to the ONI building, he demanded particulars. The lieutenant dutifully scoured his memory. "Brought in on some cloak-and-dagger deal, Commander. The kind you usually run. Lieutenant Commander Jacobi was in Syndic Territory on a recruiting, sabotage and reconnaisance mission and one of the D.A.R. passed the girl on to him. A real Syndic member. Priceless. And, as I said, she identified this fellow as Charles Orsino, another Syndic. Why are you so interested, if I may ask?"

The Commander dearly wanted to give him a grim: "You may not," but didn't dare. Now was the time to be frank and open. One hint that he had anything to hide or cover up would put his throat to the knife. "The man's my baby, Lieutenant," he said. "Either your girl's mistaken or Van Dellen and his polygraph tech and I were taken in by a brand-new technique." *That* was nice work, he congratulated himself. Got in Van Dellen and the tech . . . . Maybe, come to think of it, the tech *was* crooked? No; there was the way Wyman had responded perfectly under scop.

ONI's building was two stories and an attic, woodframed and boarded. It was beginning to rot already in the eternal Irish damp.

"We've got her on the third floor, Commander," the lieutenant said. "You get there by a ladder."

"In God's name, why?" They walked past the Charge of Quarters, who snapped to a guilty and belated attention, and through the deserted offices of the first and second floors.

"Frankly, we've had a little trouble hanging on to her."

"She runs away?"

"No, nothing like that—not yet, at least. Marine G-2 and Guard Intelligence School have both tried to snatch her from us. First with requisitions, then with muscle. We hope to keep her until the word gets to Iceland.

Then, naturally, *we'll* be out in the cold."

The lieutenant laughed at his feeble joke. Grinnel, puffing up the ladder, did not.

Lee Bennet's quarters were a solidly finished-off section of the attic. The door and lock were impressive. The lieutenant rapped on the door. "Are you awake, Lee? There's an officer here who wants to talk to you about Orsino."

"Come in," she said.

The lieutenant's hands flew over the lock and the door sprang open. The girl was sitting by the room's one window in the dark.

"I'm Commander Grinnel, my dear," he said. After eight hours in the joint, he could feel authentically fatherly to her. "If the time isn't quite convenient I can come back at your pleasure—"

"It's all right," she said listlessly. "What do you want to know?"

"The man you identify as Orsino—it was quite a shock to me. Commander Van Dellen, who died a hero's death only days ago, accepted him as authentic and so, I must admit, did I. He passed both scop and polygraph."

"I can't help that," she said. "He came right up to me and told me who he was. I recognized him, of course. He's a polo player. I've seen him play on Long Island often enough, the damned snob. He's not much in the Syndic, but he's close to F. W. Taylor. Orsino's an orphan. I don't know whether Taylor's actually adopted him or not. I think not."

"No—possible—mistake?"

"No possible mistake." She began to tremble. "My God, Commander Whoever-You-Are, do you think I could forget one of those damned sneering faces. Or what those people did to me? Get the lie-detector again! Strap me into the lie-detector! I insist on it! I won't be called a liar! Do you hear me? Get the lie-detector!"

"Please, please, please," the Commander soothed. "I do believe you, my dear. Nobody could doubt your sincerity. Thank you for helping us, and good night." He backed out of the room with the lieutenant. As the door closed he snapped at him: "Well, mister?"

The lieutenant shrugged. "The lie-detector always bears her out. We've stopped using it on her. We're convinced that she's on our side. Almost deserving of citizenship."

"Come now," the Commander said. "You know better than that." They climbed down the ladder, the Commander first, as naval etiquette prescribed.

Behind the locked door, Lee Bennet had thrown herself on the bed, dry-eyed. She wished she could cry, but tears never came. Not since those three roistering drunkards had demonstrated their virility as males and their immunity as Syndics on her . . . she couldn't cry any more.

Charles Orsino—another one of them. She hoped they caught him and killed him, slowly. She knew all this was true. Then why did she feel like a murderess? Why did she think incessantly of suicide? Why, why, why?

Dawn came imperceptibly. First Charles could discern the outline of treetops against the sky and then a little of the terrain before him and at last two twisted shadows that slowly became sprawling half-naked bodies. One of them was a woman's, mangled by fifty-caliber slugs. The other was the body of a bearded giant—the one with whom they had struggled in the dark.

Charles crawled out stiffly to inspect it. Sure enough, he had been wounded; a slug in the thigh. The woman was—had been—a stringy, white-haired crone. Some animal's skull was tied to her pate with sinews as a headdress, and she was tatooed with blue crescents. The jaygee joined him standing over her and said: "One of their witches. Part of the religion, if you can call it that."

"A brand-new religion?" Charles asked dubiously. "Made up out of whole cloth?"

"No," the jaygee said. "I understand it's an *old* religion—pre-Christian. It kept going underground until the Troubles. Then it flared up again all over Europe. A filthy business. Animal sacrifices every new moon. Human sacrifices twice a year. What can you expect from people like that?"

Charles reminded himself that the jaygee's fellow citizens boiled recalcitrant slaves. "I'll see what I can do about the jeep," he said.

The jaygee sat down on the wet grass. "What the hell's the use?" he mumbled wearily. "Even if you get it running again. Even if we get back to the base. They'll be gunning for you. Maybe they'll be gunning for me if they killed my father." He tried to smile. "You got any aces in the hole, gangster?"

"Maybe," Orsino said slowly. "What do you know about a woman named Lee—Bennet? Works with ONI?"

"Smuggled over here by the D.A.R. A gold mine of information. She's a little nuts, too. What have you got on her?"

"Does she swing any weight? *Is she a citizen?*"

"No weight. They're just using her over at Intelligence to fill out the picture of the Syndic. And she couldn't be a citizen. A woman has to marry a citizen to be naturalized. What have you got to do with her, for God's sake? Did you know her on the other side? She's death to the Syndic; she can't do anything for you."

Charles barely heard him. That had to be it. The trigger on Lee Falcaro's conditioning had to be the oath of citizenship as it was for his. And it hadn't been tripped because this pirate gang didn't particularly want or need women as first-class, all-privileges citizens. A small part of the Government's cultural complex— but one that could trap Lee Falcaro forever in the shell of her synthetic substitute for a personality. Lie-tests, yes. Scopolamine, yes. But for a woman, no subsequent oath.

Untriggered, Lee Falcaro was an unexploded bomb in the nerve center of the North American Navy. How to set her off?

He told the jaygee. "I ran into her in New Portsmouth. She knew me from the other side. She turned me in . . ." He knelt at a puddle and drank thirstily; the water eased hunger cramps a little. "I'll see what I can do with the jeep."

He lifted the hood and stole a look at the jaygee. Van Dellen was dropping off to sleep on the wet grass. Charles pried a shear pin from the jeep's winch, punched out the shear pin that had given way in the transmission and replaced it. It involved some hammering. Cracked block, he thought contemptuously. An officer, and he couldn't tell whether the block was cracked or not. If I ever get out of this we'll sweep them from the face of the earth—or more likely just get rid of their tomfool Sociocrats and Constitutionists. The rest are probably all right. Except maybe for those bastards of Guardsmen. A bad lot. Let's hope they get killed in the fighting.

The small of his back tickled; he reached around to scratch it and felt cold metal.

"Turn slowly or you'll be spitted like a pig," a bass voice growled.

He turned slowly. The cold metal, now at his chest, was the leaf-shaped blade of a spear. It was wielded by a red-haired, red-bearded, barrel-chested giant whose blue-green eyes were as cold as death.

"Tie that one," somebody said. Another half-naked man jerked his wrists behind him and lashed them together with cords.

"Hobble his feet." It was a woman's voice. A length of cord or sinew was knotted to his ankles with a foot or two of play. He could walk but not run. The giant lowered his spear and stepped aside.

The first thing Charles saw was that Lieutenant (j.g.) Van Dellen of the North American Navy had escaped forever from his doubts and confusions. They had skewered him to the turf while he slept. Charles hoped he had not felt the blow, and it was likely. The shock-power of a broad-bladed spear must be immense.

The second thing he saw was a supple and coltish girl of perhaps twenty tenderly removing the animal skull from the head of the slain witch and knotting it to her own red-tressed head. Even to Orsino's numbed understanding, it was clearly an act of the highest significance. It subtly changed the composition of the six-man group in the little glade. They had been a small mob until she put on the skull, but the moment she did they moved instinctively—one a step or two, the other merely turning a bit, perhaps—to orient on her. There was no doubt that she was in charge.

A witch, Orsino thought. "It kept going underground until the Troubles . . . . A filthy business—human sacrifices twice a year."

She approached him and, like the shifting of a kaleidoscope, the group fell into a new pattern of which she was still the focus. Charles thought he had never seen a face so humorlessly conscious of power. The petty ruler of a few barbarians, she carried herself as though she were empress of the universe. Nor did a large gray louse that crawled from her hairline across her forehead and back again affect her in the slightest. She wore a greasy animal hide as though it were royal purple. It added up to either insanity or a limitless pretension to religious authority. And her eyes were not mad.

"You," she said coldly. "What about the jeep and the guns? Do they go?"

He laughed suddenly and idiotically at these words from the mouth of a stone-age goddess. A raised spear sobered him instantly. "Yes," he said, "yes—uh, miss."

"Show my men how," she said, and squatted regally on the turf.

"Please," he said, "could I have something to eat first?"

She nodded indifferently and one of the men loped off into the brush.

His hands untied and his face greasy with venison fat, Charles spent the daylight hours instructing six savages in the nomenclature, maintenance and operation of the jeep and the twin-fifty machine gun.

They absorbed it with utter lack of curiosity. He could have told them that there were little green men in the brass cartridge cases who got angry when goosed by the primer and kicked the bullets out with their little feet. They more or less learned to start and steer and stop the jeep. They more or less learned to load and aim and fire the gun.

Through the lessons the girl sat absolutely motionless, first in shadow, then in noon and afternoon sun, and then in shadow again. But she had been listening. She said at last: "You are telling them nothing new now. Is there no more?"

Charles noted that a spear was poised at his ribs. "A great deal more," he said hastily. "It takes months."

"They can work them now. What more is there to learn?"

"Well, what to do if something goes wrong."

She said, as though speaking from vast experience: "When something goes wrong, you start over again. That is all you can do. When I make death-wine for the spear blades and the death-wine does not kill, it is because something went wrong—a word or a sign or picking a plant at the wrong time. The only thing to do is make the poison again. As you grow in experience you make fewer mistakes. That is how it will be with my men when they work the jeep and the guns."

She nodded ever so slightly at one of the men and he took a firmer grip on his spear.

"No!" Charles exploded. "You don't understand! This isn't like anything you do at all!" He was sweating, even in the late afternoon chill. "You've got to have somebody who knows how to repair the jeep and the gun. If they're busted they're busted and no a-mount of starting over again will make them work!"

She nodded and said: "We'll take him with us." Charles was torn between relief and wonder at the way she spoke. He realized that he had never, literally *never*, seen any person concede a point in quite that fashion. There had been no hesitation, there had been no reluctance in the voice, not a flicker of displeasure in the face. Simply, without forcing, she had said: "We'll take him with us." It was as though—as though she had remade the immediate past, unmaking her opposition to the idea, nullifying it. She was a person who was not at war with herself in any respect whatever, a person who knew exactly who she was and what she was—

"Awk!" said Charles, strangling. Two of the sourfaced spearmen were efficiently clamping a rustic yoke around his neck; two five-foot saplings tied together with sinews at each end, the ties out of arm's reach. They were sprung apart, enough to give him neck room, by two notched sticks. His eyes bugged when, as a finishing touch, the spearmen tied his wrists to the notched sticks.

The girl rose in a single flowing motion, startling after her day spent in immobility. She led the way, flanked by two of the spearmen. The other four followed in the jeep, at a crawl. Last of all came Charles, and nobody had to urge him. In his portable trap his hours would be numbered if he got separated from his captors.

Stick with them, he told himself, stumbling through the brush. Just stay alive and you can outsmart savages. His yoke whacked up against a pair of trees; he cursed, backed, turned his head and stumbled on after the growl of the jeep.

Dawn brought them to journey's end, a collection of mud-and-wattle huts, a corral enclosing a few dozen head of wretched diseased cattle, a few adults and a few children. The girl was still clear-eyed and supple in her movements. Her spearmen yawned and stretched stiffly. Charles was a walking dead man, battered by countless trees and stumbles on the long trek. With red and swollen eyes he watched while half-naked brats swarmed over the jeep and grownups made obeisances to the girl—all but one.

This was an evil-faced harridan who said to her with cool insolence: "I see you claim the power of the goddess now, my dear. Has something happened to my sister?"

"The guns killed a certain person. I put on the skull. You know what I am; do not say 'claim to be.' I warn you once."

"Liar!" shrieked the harridan. "You killed her and stole the skull! St. Patrick and St. Bridget shrivel your guts! Abaddon and Lucifer pierce your eyes!"

An arena formed about them as the girl said coldly: "I warn you the second time."

The harridan made obscure signs with her fingers, glaring at her; there was a moan from the watchers; some turned aside and a half-grown girl fainted dead away.

The girl with the skull on her pate said, as though speaking from a million years and a million miles away: "This is the third warning; there are no more. Now the worm is in your backbone gnawing. Now the maggots are at your eyes, devouring them. Your bowels turn to water; your heart pounds like the heart of a bird; soon it will not beat at all." As the eerie, space-filling whisper drilled on the watchers broke and ran, holding their hands over their ears, white-faced, but the harridan stood as if rooted to the earth. Charles listened dully as the curse was droned, nor was he surprised when the harridan fell, blasted by it. Another sorceress, aided it is true by Seconal, had months ago done the same to him.

The people trickled back, muttering and abject. A small boy was the first to spurn the body of the defeated pretender, with a self-conscious, "look-how-loyal-I-am" glance at the witch-girl. Others followed suit while she watched impassively. Charles turned away, sickened, as hysteria mounted by imperceptible degrees and the body was kicked to bloody rags. But he could not shut the vengeful yells from his ears.

Just stay alive and you can outsmart these savages, he repeated ironically to himself. It had dawned on him that these savages lived by an obscure and complicated code that must be harder to master than the intricacies of the Syndic or the Government.

A kick roused him to his feet. One of the spearmen grunted: "I'm putting you with Kennedy. I guess you know him."

"No."

"No? You come from Portsmouth, he comes from Portsmouth. How come you don't know him?" He wore a suspicious scowl.

"All right," Charles groaned, "maybe I know him. Can you take this thing off me?"

"Later." He prodded Charles to a minute, ugly blockhouse of logs from which came smoke and an irregular metallic clanging. He cut the yoke off Charles' neck, rolled great boulders away from a crawl-hole and shoved him through.

The place was about six by nine feet, hemmed in by ten-inch logs. The light was very bad and the smell was too. A few loopholes let in some air. There was a latrine pit and an open stone hearth and a naked brown man with wild hair and a beard.

Rubbing his neck, Charles asked uncertainly: "Are you Kennedy?"

The man looked up and croaked after a long pause: "Are you from the Government?"

"Yes," Charles said, hope slowly rekindling. "Thank God they put us together. There's a jeep they brought in with me, and plenty miles in the tank left. Also a twin-fifty. If we play this right the two of us can bust out—"

He stopped, disconcerted. Kennedy had turned to the hearth and the small, fierce fire glowing on it and began to pound a red-hot lump of metal. There were spearheads and arrowheads about in various stages of completion, as well as files and a hone.

"What's the matter?" he demanded. "Aren't you interested?"

"Of course I'm interested," Kennedy said. "But we've got to begin at the beginning. You're too *general*." His voice was mild, but reproving.

"You're right," Charles said. "I guess you've made a try or two yourself. But now that there are two of us, what do you suggest? Can you drive a jeep? Can you fire a twin-fifty?"

The man poked the lump of metal into the

heart of the fire again, picked up a black-scaled spearhead and began to file an edge into it. "Let's get down to essentials," he suggested apologetically. "What is escape? Getting from an undesirable place to a desirable place, opposing and neutralizing things or persons adverse to the change of state in the process. But I'm not being specific, am I? Let's say, then, escape is getting *us* from a relatively undesirable place to a relatively desirable place, opposing and neutralizing the aborigines." He put aside the file and reached for the hone, sleeking it along the bright metal ribbon of the new edge. He looked up with a pleased smile and asked: "How's it for a plan?"

"Fine," Charles muttered. Kennedy beamed proudly as he repeated: "Fine, fine," and sank to the ground, borne down by the almost physical weight of his depression. His hoped-for ally was stark mad.

THIRTEEN

Kennedy turned out to have been an armorer-artificer of the North American Navy, captured two years ago while deerhunting too far from the logging-camp road to New Portsmouth. Fed on scraps of gristle, isolated from his kind, beaten when he failed to make his daily quota of spearheads and arrowpoints, he had shyly retreated into beautifully interminable labyrinths of abstraction. Now and then, Charles Orsino got a word or two of sense from him before the rosy clouds closed in again on his mind. When attempted conversation with the lunatic palled, Charles could watch the aborigines through chinks in the palisade. There were about fifty of them. There would have been more if they hadn't been given to infanticide—for what reason, Charles could not guess. It was not lack of food. Hunting was good, potatoes were in the ground for the digging, and they had their cattle.

He had been there a week when the boulders were rolled away one morning and he was roughly called out. He said to Kennedy before stooping to crawl through the hold: "Take it easy, friend. I'll be back, I hope."

Kennedy looked up with a puzzled smile: "That's such a *general* statement, Charles. Exactly what are you implying—"

Charles shrugged helplessly and crawled through.

The witch-girl was there, flanked as always by spearmen. She said abruptly: "I have been listening to you. Why are you untrue to your brothers?"

He gawked. The only thing that seemed to fit was: "That's such a *general* statement," but he didn't say it.

"Answer," one of the spearmen growled.

"I—I don't understand. I have no brothers."

"Your brothers in Portsmouth, on the sea. Whatever you call them, they are your brothers, all children of the mother called Government. Why are you untrue to them?"

He began to understand. "They aren't my brothers. I'm not a child of the Government. I'm a child of another mother far away, on the other side of the ocean, called Syndic."

She looked puzzled—and almost human—for an instant. Then the visor dropped over her face again as she said: "That is true. Now there is some work for you. You must teach a certain person the jeep and the guns. Teach her well. See that she gets her hands on the metal and into the grease. See that she truly learns how to work the jeep and the guns." To a spearman she said: "Bring Martha."

The spearman brought Martha, who was trying not to cry. She was a half-naked child of ten!

The witch-girl abruptly left them. Her guards took Martha and bewildered Charles to the edge of the village where the jeep and its mounted guns stood behind a silly little museum-exhibit rope of vine. Feathers and bones were knotted into the vine. The spearmen treated it as though it were a high-tension transmission line.

"You break it," one of them said edgily to Charles. He did, and the spearmen sighed with relief. Martha stopped scowling and stared, round-eyed, alternately at him and the bedecked vine trailing in the dust.

"He's still standing up," she said to one of the men.

"That's because he's from outside," the spearman said. "Don't you know anything, girl? With somebody from outside you can't use the power of the goddess. You have to use *this*." He brandished his spear and pinked Charles lightly in the left buttock. Everybody roared with laughter, including the little girl. In the middle of it she remembered some private grief and tears almost came.

The spearman said to Charles: "Go ahead and teach her. The firing pins are out of the guns, and if you try to start the jeep you get a spear through you. Now teach her." He and the rest squatted on the turf around the jeep. The little girl shied violently as he took her hand, and tried to run away. One of the spearmen caught her without effort and slung her back into the circle. She brushed against the jeep and froze, white-faced.

"Martha," Charles said patiently, "there's nothing to be afraid of. The guns won't go off and the jeep won't move. I'll teach you how to work them so you can kill everybody you don't like with the guns and go faster than a deer in the jeep—"

He was talking into empty air as far as the child was concerned. She was muttering, staring at the arm that had brushed the jeep: "That did it, I guess. There goes the power. May the goddess blast her—no. The power's out of me now. I felt it go." She looked up at Charles, quite calmly, and said: "Go on. Show me all about it. Do a good job."

"Martha, what are you talking about?"

"She was afraid of me, my sister, so she's robbing me of the power. Don't you know? I guess not. The goddess hates iron and machines. I had the power of the goddess in me, but it's gone now; I felt it go. Now nobody'll be afraid of me any more." Her face contorted and she said: "Show me how you work the guns."

He taught her what he could while the circle of spearmen looked on and grinned, cracking raw jokes about the child as anybody, anywhere, would about a tyrant deposed. She pretended to ignore them, grimly repeating names after him and imitating his practiced movements in loading drill. She was very bright, Charles realized. When he got a chance he muttered, "I'm sorry about this, Martha. It isn't my idea."

She whispered bleakly: "I know. I liked you. I was sorry when the other outsider took your dinner." She began to sob uncontrollably. "I'll never see anything again! Nobody'll ever be afraid of me again!" She buried her face against Charles' shoulder.

He smoothed her tangled hair mechanically and said to the watching, grinning circle: "Look, hasn't this gone far enough? Haven't you got what you wanted?"

The headman stretched and spat and mounted the jeep. "Guess so," he said. "Come on, girl." He yanked Martha from the seat and booted her toward the huts of the village.

Charles scrambled down just ahead of a dig in the rump from a spear. He let himself be led back to the smithy blockhouse and shoved through the crawl-hole.

"I was thinking about what you said the other day," Kennedy beamed, rasping a file over an arrowhead. "When I said that to change one molecule in the past you'd have to change *every* molecule in the past, and you said, 'Maybe so,' I've figured that what you were driving at was—"

"Kennedy," Charles said, "please shut up just this once. I've got to think."

"In what sense do you mean that, Charles? Do you mean that you're a rational animal and therefore that your *being* rather than *essence* is—"

"Shut up or I'll pick up a rock and bust your head in with it!" Charles roared, and he more than half meant it. Kennedy hunched down

before his hearth looking offended and scared. Charles squatted with his head in his hands.

I have been listening to you.

Repeated drives of the Government to wipe out the aborigines. Drives that never succeeded.

I'll never see anything again.

The way the witch-girl had blasted her rival —but that was suggestion. But—

I have been listening to you. Why are you untrue to your brothers?

He'd said nothing like that to anybody, not to her or poor Kennedy.

He thought vaguely of *psi* force, a fragment in his memory. An old superstition, like the id-ego-superego triad of the sick-minded psychologists. Like vectors of the mind, exploded nonsense. But—

I have been listening to you. Why are you untrue to your brothers?

Charles smacked one fist against the sand floor in impotent rage. He was going as crazy as Kennedy. Did the witch-girl—and Martha— have hereditary *psi* power? He mocked himself savagely: That's such a *general* question!

Neurotic adolescent girls in kerosene-lit farmhouses, he thought vaguely. Things that go bump—and crash and blooie and *whoo-oo-oo!* in the night. Not in electric-lit city apartments. Not around fleshed-up middle-aged men and women. You take a hyperthyroid virgin, isolate her from power machinery and electric fields, put on the pressures that make her feel alone and tense to the bursting point

—and, naturally enough, something bursts. A chamber pot sails from under the bed and shatters on the skull of step-father-tyrant. The wide-gilt-framed portrait of thundergod-grandfather falls with a crash. Sure, the nail crystallized and broke—*who crystallized it?*

Neurotic adolescent girls speaking in tongues, reading face-down cards and closed books, over and over again screaming aloud when sister or mother dies in a railroad wreck fifty miles away, of cancer a hundred miles away, in a bombing overseas.

Sometimes they made saints of them— Thérèse of Lisieux. Sometimes they burned them—countless witches. Sometimes they burned them and *then* made saints of them —Joan, with her voices and visions.

A blood-raw hunk of venison came sailing through one of the loopholes and flopped on the sand.

I was sorry when the other outsider took your dinner.

That had been three days ago. He'd dozed off while Kennedy broiled the meat over the hearth. When he woke, Kennedy had gobbled it all and was whimpering with apprehension. But he'd done nothing and said nothing; the man wasn't responsible. He'd said nothing, and yet somehow the child knew about it.

His days were numbered; soon enough the jeep would be out of gas and the guns would be out of ammo or an unreplaceable part lost or broken. Then, according to the serene logic that ruled the witch-girl, he'd be surplus.

But there was a key to it somehow.

He got up and slapped Kennedy's hand away from the venison. "Naughty," he said, and divided it equally with a broad spearblade.

"Naughty," Kennedy said morosely. "The naught-class, the null-class. I'm the null-class. I plus the universe equal one, the universe-class. If you could transpose—but you can't transpose." Silently they toasted their venison over the fire.

It was a moonless night with one great planet, Jupiter he supposed, reigning over the star-powdered sky. Kennedy slept muttering feebly in the corner. The hearth fire was out. It had to be out by dark. The spearmen took no chance of their trying to burn down the place. The village had long since gone to sleep, campfires doused, skin flaps pulled to across the door holes. From the corral one of the spavined, tick-ridden cows mooed uneasily and then fell silent.

Charles then began the hardest job of his life. He tried to think, straight and uninter-rupted, of Martha, the little girl. Some of the things that interrupted him were:

The remembered smell of fried onions; they didn't have onions here;

Salt;

I wonder how the old 101st Precinct's getting along;

The fellow who wanted to get married on a hundred dollars;

Lee Falcaro, damn her!

This is damn foolishness; it can't possibly work;

Poor old Kennedy;

I'll starve before I eat another mouthful of that greasy deermeat;

The Van Dellen kid, I wonder if I could have saved him;

Reiner's right; we've got to clean up the Government and then try to civilize these people;

There must be something wrong with my head; I can't seem to concentrate;

That terrific third-chukker play in the Finals, my picture all over town;

Would Uncle Frank laugh at this?

It was hopeless. He sat bolt upright, his eyes squeezed tensely together, trying to visualize the child and call her and it couldn't be done. Skittering images of her zipped through his mind, only to be shoved aside. It was damn foolishness, anyway . . . .

He unkinked himself, stretched and lay down on the sand floor thinking bitterly: Why try? You'll be dead in a few days or a few weeks; kiss the world good-by. Back in Syndic Territory, fat, sloppy, happy Syndic Territory, did they know how good they had it? He wished he could tell them to cling to their good life. But Uncle Frank said it didn't do any good to cling; it was a matter of tension and relaxation. When you stiffen up a way of life and try to fossilize it so it'll stay that way forever, then you find you've lost it.

Little Martha wouldn't understand it. Magic, ritual, the power of the goddess, fear of iron, fear of the jeep's vine enclosure—

cursed, no doubt—what went on in such a mind? Could she throw things like a poltergeist-girl? They didn't have 'em any more; maybe it had something to do with electric fields or even iron. Or were they all phonies? An upset adolescent girl is a hell of a lot likelier to fake phenomena than produce them. Little Martha hadn't been faking her despair, though. The witch-girl—her sister, wasn't she?—didn't fake her icy calm and power. Martha'd be better off without such stuff—

"Charles," a whisper said.

He muttered stupidly: "My God. She heard me," and crept to the palisade. Through a chink between the logs she was just visible in the starlight.

She whispered: "I thought I wasn't going to see anything or hear anything ever again but I sat up and I heard you calling and you said you wanted to help me if I'd help you so I came as fast as I could without waking anybody up—you *did* call me, didn't you?"

"Yes, I did. Martha, do you want to get out of here? Go far away with me?"

"You bet I do. *She's* going to take the power of the goddess out of me and marry me to Dinny, he stinks like a goat and he has a cock-eye, and then she'll kill all our babies. Just tell me what to do and I'll do it." She sounded very grim and decided.

"Can you roll the boulders away from the hole there?" He was thinking vaguely of teleportation; each boulder was a two-man job.

She said no.

He snarled: "Then why did you bother to come here?"

"Don't talk like that to me," the child said sharply—and he remembered what she thought she was.

"Sorry," he said.

"What I came about," she said calmly, "was the ex-plosion. Can you make an ex-plosion like you said? Back there at the jeep?"

What in God's name was she talking about?

"Back there," she said with exaggerated patience, "you was thinking about putting all the cartridges together and blowing up the whole damn shebang. Remember?"

He did, vaguely. One of a hundred schemes that had drifted through his head. It had caught her fancy.

"I'd sure like to see that ex-plosion," she said. "The way *she* got things figured, I'd almost just as soon get exploded myself as not."

"I might blow up the logs here and get out," he said slowly. "I think you'd be a mighty handy person to have along, too. Can you get me about a hundred of the machine-gun cartridges?"

"They'll miss 'em."

"Sneak me a few at a time. I'll empty them, put them together again and you sneak them back."

She said, slow and troubled: "*She* set the power of the goddess to guard them."

"Listen to me, Martha," he said. "I mean *listen*. You'll be doing it for me and they told you the power of the goddess doesn't work on outsiders. Isn't that right?"

There was a long pause, and she said at last with a sigh: "I sure wish I could see your eyes, Charles. I'll try it, but I'm damned if I would if Dinny didn't stink so bad." She slipped away and Charles tried to follow her with his mind through the darkness, to the silly little rope of vine with the feathers and bones knotted in it —but he couldn't. Too tense again.

Kennedy stirred and muttered complainingly as an icy small breeze cut through the chinks of the palisade, whispering.

Charles' eyes, tuned to the starlight, picked up Martha bent almost double, creeping toward the smithy-prison. She wore a belt of fifty-caliber cartridges around her neck like a stole. Looked like about a dozen of them. He hastily scooped out a bowl of clean sand and whispered: "Any trouble?"

He couldn't see the grin on her face, but knew it was there. "It was easy," she bragged. "One bad minute and then I checked with you and it was okay."

"Good kid. Can you get the belt through between these logs? I guess not. Pull the cartridges out of the links the way I showed you and pass them through one at a time."

She did. It was a tight squeeze. He hoped it wouldn't scar the wood and start people thinking in the daytime.

Dubiously, he fingered one of the cartridges. The bullet seemed to be awfully well seated. He bit down on the bullet and tried to wobble it out of the neck. The bullet didn't wobble; his teeth did. He spat out the taste of oil and crept to the hearth, carrying the cartridge. He tried a spearhead's socket; it was too big. The bullet fitted nicely into the socket of an arrowhead, but the arrowhead didn't give him enough leverage. The hell with it; he had to work with what he had. He jammed the bullet into the socket and wrenched at the arrowhead with thumb and forefinger—all he could get into it. His hand was numb with cramp and bleeding by the time the brass neck began to spread. He dumped the powder into his little basin in the sand and reseated the bullet.

Charles shifted hands on the second cartridge. On the third he realized that he could put the point of the bullet on a hearthstone and press on the neck with both thumbs. It went faster then; in perhaps an hour he was passing the reassembled cartridges back through the palisade.

"Time for another load?" he asked.

"Nope," the girl said. "Tomorrow night."

"Good kid."

She giggled. "It's going to be a hell of a big bang, ain't it, Charles?"

FOURTEEN

"Leave the fire alone," Charles said sharply to Kennedy. The little man was going to douse it for the night.

There was a flash of terrified sense from the lunatic: "They beat you," he said. "If the fire's on after dark they beat you. Fire and dark are equal and opposite." He began to smile. "Fire is the negative of dark. You just change the sign, in effect rotate it through 180 degrees. But to rotate it through 180 degrees you have to first rotate it through one degree. And to rotate it through one degree you first have to rotate it through half a degree." He was beaming now, having forgotten all about the fire. Charles banked it with utmost care, heaping a couple of flat stones for a chimney that would preserve the life of one glowing coal invisibly.

He stretched out on the sand, one hand on the little heap beneath which five pounds of smokeless powder was buried. Kennedy continued to drone out his power-series happily, apparently having forgotten what he had started to demonstrate. He usually did.

Through the chinks in the palisade a man's profile showed against the twilight. "Shut up, you fool," he said contemptuously, but Kennedy didn't hear him. A spear darted through between two logs and dug a quarter-inch into Kennedy's stringy thigh. The lunatic howled and the spearman laughed. "Shut up. The fire's out? Go to sleep. Work tomorrow."

Kennedy, shivering, rolled over and muttered to himself. The spear darted at him again, playfully, but it didn't reach. The spearman laughed and went on.

Charles hardly saw the byplay. His whole mind was concentrated on the spark beneath the improvised chimney. He had left such a spark seven nights running. Only twice had it lived more than an hour. Tonight—tonight, it *had* to last. Tonight was the last night of the witch-girl's monthly courses, and during them she lost—or thought she lost, which was the same thing—the power of the goddess.

Primitive aborigines, he peered silently at himself. A lifetime wasn't long enough to learn the intricacies of their culture—as occasional executions among them for violating magical law proved to the hilt. His first crude notion—blowing the palisade apart and running like hell—was replaced by a complex escape plan hammered out in detail between him and Martha.

Martha assured him that the witch-girl

could track him through the dark by the
power of the goddess except for four days a
month—and he believed it. Martha herself did
not yet suffer from this limitation, and she
laid a matter-of-fact claim to keener second
sight than her sister because of her virginity.
With Martha to guide him through the night
and the witch-girl's power disabled, they'd get
a day's head start. His hand strayed to a
pebble under which jerked venison was
hidden and ready.

"But Martha, are you sure you're not—not
kidding yourself? Are you *sure?*"

He felt her grin on the other side of the
palisade. "You're sure wishing Uncle Frank
was here so you could ask him about it, don't
you, Charles? You sure think a lot of him."

He sure was. He sure did. He wiped his
brow, suddenly clammy.

Kennedy couldn't come along, for two reasons. One, he wasn't responsible. Two, he
might have to be Charles' cover-story. They
weren't too dissimilar in build, age, or color-
ing. Charles had a beard by now that suf-
ficiently obscured his features, and two years'
absence should have softened recollections of
Kennedy. Interrogated, Charles could take
refuge in an imitation of Kennedy's lunacy.
And there would be Martha. If the worst came
to the worst, she'd tip him off and he would
have the poor satisfaction of going down
fighting.

"Charles, the one thing I don't get is this Lee
dame. She got a spell on her? You don't want
to mess with that."

"Listen, Martha, we've *got* to mess with her. It isn't a spell—exactly. Anyway I know how to take it off and then she'll be on our side. And we've got to go into New Portsmouth. There's more water to cross than you ever saw or heard of or dreamed of and the people at New Portsmouth have the only boats that'll do it."

"Can I set off the explosion? If you let me set off the explosion, I'll quit my bitching."

"We'll see," he said.

She chuckled very faintly in the dark. "Okay," she told him. "If I can't, I can't."

He thought of being married to a woman who could spot your smallest lie or reservation, and shuddered.

Kennedy was snoring by now and twilight was deepening into blackness. There was a quarter-moon, obscured by overcast. He hitched along the sand and peered through a chink at a tiny noise. It was the small scuffling feet of a woods rat racing through the grass from one morsel of food to the next. It never reached it. There was a soft rush of wings as a great dark owl plummeted to earth and struck talons into the brown fur. The rat squealed its life away while the owl lofted silently to a tree branch where it stood on one leg, swaying drunkenly and staring with huge yellow eyes.

As sudden as that, it'll be, Charles thought, abruptly weighted with despair. A half-crazy kid and yours truly trying to outsmart and out-tarzan these wild men. If only the little dope would let me take the jeep! But the jeep was out. She rationalized her retention of the power even after handling iron by persuading herself that she was only acting for Charles; there was some obscure precedent in a long, memorized poem which served her as a text-book of magic. But riding in the jeep was *out*.

By now she should be stringing magic vines across some of the huts and trails. "They'll see 'em when they get torches and it'll scare 'em bad. Of course I don't know how to do it right, but they don't know that. It'll slow 'em down. If *she* comes out of her house—and maybe she won't—she'll know they don't matter and send the men after us. But we'll be on our way. Charles, you *sure* I can't set off the explosion? Yeah, I guess you are. Maybe I can set off one when we get to New Portsmouth?"

"If I can possibly arrange it."

She sighed: "I guess that'll have to do."

It was too silent; he couldn't bear it. With feverish haste he uncovered the caches of powder and meat. Under the sand was a fat clayey soil. He dug up handfuls of it, wet it with the only liquid available and worked it into paste. He felt his way to the logs decided on for blasting, dug out a hole at their bases in the clay. After five careful trips from the powder cache to the hole, the mine was filled. He covered it with clay and laid on a roof of flat stones from the hearth. The spark of fire still glowed, and he nursed it with twigs.

She was there, whispering: "Charles?"

"Right here. Everything set?"

"All set. Let's have that ex-plosion."

He took the remaining powder and, with minute care, laid a train across the stockade to the mine. He crouched into a ball and flipped a burning twig onto the black line that crossed the white sand floor.

The blast seemed to wake up the world. Kennedy charged out of sleep, screaming, and a million birds woke with a squawk. Charles was conscious more of the choking reek than the noise as he scooped up the jerked venison and rushed through the ragged gap in the wall. His skin felt peppered; he had caught some splinters or loose dirt. A hand caught his—a small hand.

"You're groggy," Martha's voice said, sounding far away. "Come on—fast. *Man*, that was a great ex-plosion!"

She towed him through the woods and underbrush—fast. As long as he hung on to her he didn't stumble or run into a tree once. Irrationally embarrassed by his dependence on a child, he tried letting go for a short time —very short—and was quickly battered into changing his mind. He thought dizzily of the spearmen trying to follow through the dark and could almost laugh again.

Their trek to the coast was marked by desperate speed. For twenty-four hours, they stopped only to gnaw at their rations or snatch a drink at a stream. Charles kept moving because it was unendurable to let a ten-year-old girl exceed him in stamina. Both of them paid terribly for the murderous pace they kept. The child's face became skull-like and her eyes red; her lips dried and cracked. He gasped at her as they pulled their way up a bramble-covered forty-five degree slope: "How do you do it? Isn't this ever going to end?"

"Ends soon," she croaked at him. "You know we dodged 'em three times?"

He could only shake his head.

She stared at him with burning red eyes. "This ain't hard," she croaked. "You do this with a gutful of poison, *that's* hard."

"*Did* you?"

She grinned crookedly and chanted something he did not understand:

"Nine moons times thirteen is the
    daughter's age
When she drinks the death-cup.
Three leagues times three she must race
    and rage
Down hills and up—"

She added matter-of-factly: "Last year. Prove I have the power of the goddess. Run, climb, with your guts falling out. This year, starve for a week and run down a deer of seven points."

Charles thought dully that the power of the goddess was dearly bought at the price.

He had lost track of days and nights when they stood on the brow of a hill at dawn and looked over the sea. The girl gasped: "'Sall right now. *She* wouldn't let them go. She's a bitch, but she's no fool." The child fell in her tracks. Charles, too tired for panic, felt her

pulse and decided she had simply fallen
asleep where she stood. He slept too.

Charles woke with a wonderful smell in his
nostrils. He followed it hungrily down the re-
verse slope of the hill to a curious rock forma-
tion—two great slabs upright and a third
across them as a lintel, forming a Greek letter
pi and the whole almost covered over with
centuries of earth and vegetation. He might
have searched his memory and learned that it
was an ancient burial dolmen, but the smell
crowded out everything else.

Martha was crouched over a fire on which
rocks were heating. Beside it was a bark pot
smeared with clay. As he watched, she lifted a
red-hot rock with two green sticks and rolled
it into the pot. It boiled up and continued to
boil for an astonishing number of minutes.
That was the source of the smell.

"Breakfast?" he asked unbelievingly.

"Rabbit stew," she said. "Plenty of run-
ways, plenty of bark, plenty of green branches. I made snares. Two tough old bucks,
cooking in there for an hour."

They chewed the meat from the bones in silence. She said at last: "We can't settle down
here. Too near to the coast. And if we move
further inland, there's *her*. And others. I been
thinking." She spat a string of tough meat out.
"There's England. Work our way around the
coast. Make a raft or steal a canoe and cross
the water. *Then* we could settle down. You
can't have me for three times thirteen moons
yet or I'd lose the power. But I guess we can

wait. I heard about England and the English. They have no hearts left. We can take as many slaves as we want. They cry a lot but they don't fight. And none of their women has the power." She looked up anxiously. "You wouldn't want one of their women, would you? Not if you could have somebody with the power just by waiting for her?"

He looked down the hill and said slowly: "You know that's not what I had in mind, Martha. I have my own place with people far away. I want to get back there. I thought—I thought you'd like it too." Her face twisted. He couldn't bear to go on, not in words. "Look into my mind, Martha," he said. "Maybe you'll see what it means to me."

She stared long and deep. At last she rose, her face inscrutable, and spat into the fire. "Think I saved you for that?" she asked. "And for her? Not me. Save yourself from now on, mister. I'm going to beat my way south around the coast. England for me, and I don't want any part of you. I'd shrivel your guts with a curse if it worked on you crazy out-landers."

She strode off down the hill, gaunt and ragged, but with arrogance in her swinging, space-eating gait. Charles sat looking after her, stupefied, until she had melted into the underbrush. *Think I saved you for that? And for her?* She'd made some kind of mistake. He got up stiffly and ran after her, but he could not pick up an inch of her woodswise trail. Charles slowly climbed to the dolmen again and sat in its shelter. The bark pot's clay daubing had given way at a corner and the water had leaked out; grease coated the inside of the crude vessel. The fire was out, and he realized that he didn't have any notion of how she had started it. She had snared rabbits. How? Where? What did a snare look like and how did you make one? How did you tell a rabbit-run? He had better learn—fast.

Charles spent the morning trying to concoct simple springs out of bark strips and whippy branches. He got nowhere. The branches broke or wouldn't bend far enough. The bark shredded, or wouldn't hold a knot. Without metal, he couldn't shape the trigger to fit the bow so that it would be both sensitive and reliable.

At noon he drank enormously from a spring and looked morosely for plants that might be edible. He decided on something with a bulbous, onion-like root. For a couple of hours after that he propped rocks on sticks here and there. When he stepped back and surveyed them, he decided that any rabbit he caught with them would be, even for a rabbit, feeble-minded.

Through it all he resolutely refused to think of the basic jam he was in, trapped between the tarzans of the interior and the Government of the coast, both thirsting for his blood.

First he felt a slight intestinal qualm and then a far from slight nausea. Then the root he had eaten took over with drastic thoroughness. He collapsed, retching, and only after the first spasms had passed was he able to crawl to the dolmen. The shelter it offered was mostly psychological, but he had need of that. Under the ancient, mossy stones, he raved with delirium until dark. There were intervals when he thought a cool hand pressed wet leaves on his head and others when the leaves seemed to be burning.

Sometimes he was back in Syndic Territory, Charles Orsino of the two-goal handicap and the flashing smile. Sometimes he was back in the stinking blockhouse with Kennedy spinning interminable, excruciatingly boring strands of iridescent logic. Sometimes he was back in the psychology laboratory with the pendulum beating, the light blinking, the bell ringing and sense-impressions flooding him and drowning him with lies. Sometimes he raced in panic down the streets of New Portsmouth with sweatered Guardsmen pounding after him, their knives flashing fire.

But at last he was under the dolmen again, with Martha sponging his head and cursing him in a low, fluent undertone for being seven times seven kinds of fool.

She said tartly as recognition came into his eyes: "Yes, for the fifth time, I'm back. I should be making my way to England and a band of my own, but I'm back and I don't know why. I heard you in pain and I thought it served you right for not knowing deathroot when you see it, but I turned around and came back."

"Don't go," he said hoarsely.

She held a bark cup to his lips and made him choke down some nauseating brew. "Don't worry," she told him bitterly. "I won't go. I'll do everything you want, which shows that I'm as big a fool as you are, or bigger because I know better. I'll help you find her and take the spell off her. And may the goddess help me because I can't help myself."

He was cured in a day, and promptly found himself in the domestic's role, cooking and gutting and clearing away. But what she did was more important. She would lie relaxed in the mossy vault of the dolmen for hours on end, her breathing shallow, speaking occasionally in a whisper that was hard to catch. It was rambling and disconnected; Charles' job was to connect it up, relating the part to the whole, identifying this thought with that face, this vessel with that captain.

" . . . things like sawed tree-trunks, shells you call them . . . pointed with green crosses painted on the tips, a pile of them . . . he looks at them and he thinks they're going bad and they ought to be used soon . . . under a wooden roof they are . . . a thin man with death on his face and hate in his heart . . . he wears blue and gold . . . he sticks the gold, it's a broad band on his wrist, you call a coat's wrist the cuff, he sticks the cuff under the nose of a fellow and yells his hate out at him and the fellow feels ready to strangle on his own blood . . . it's about a boat that sank . . . no, it's about a boat that floats . . . this fellow, he's a fat little man and he kills and kills, he'd kill the man if he could . . ."

A picket boat steamed by the coast twice a day, north after dawn and south before sunset. They had to watch out for it; it swept the coast with powerful glasses.

" . . . it's the man with the bellyache again but now he's sleepy . . . he's cursing the skipper . . . he should clean his glass but he doesn't . . . sure there's nothing on the coast to trouble us . . . eight good men aboard and that one bastard of a skipper . . ."

Sometimes it jumped erratically, like an optical lever disturbed by the weight of a hair.

" . . . board over the door painted with a circle, a zigzag on its side, an up-and-down line . . . they call it office of intelligent navels . . . the lumber camp . . . machine goes chug-rip, chug-rip . . . and the place where they cut metal like wood on machines that spin around . . . a deathly sick little fellow loaded down and chained . . . fell on his face, he can't get up, his bowels are water, his muscles are stiff, like dry branches and he's afraid . . . they curse him, they beat him, they take him to a machine that spins . . . *they . . . they—they—*"

She sat bolt upright, screaming. Her eyes didn't see Charles. He drew back one hand and slammed it across her cheek in a slap that reverberated like a pistol shot. Her head rocked to the blow and her eyes snapped back from infinity-focus.

She never told Charles what they had done to the sick slave in the machine shop, and he never asked her. She went back into the trance state again after eating, but was uncertain and erratic for a day and a half, doubting her own vision and obscuring what it saw with symbols. A snarling, bloody fight between two dogs on a desk in BuPers baffled Charles until he realized that it was actually a bitter quarrel between two junior officers. Eventually the censor relaxed.

Without writing equipment, for crutches, Charles doubted profoundly that he'd be able to hang onto any of the material she supplied. He surprised himself; his memory developed with exercise.

The shadowy ranks of the New Portsmouth personnel became solider daily in his mind; the chronically fatigued ordnancemen whose mainspring was to get by with the smallest possible effort; the sex-obsessed little man in Intelligence who lived only for the brothels where he selected older women—women who looked like his mother; the human weasel in BuShips who was impotent in bed and a lacerating tyrant in the office; the admiral who knew he was dying and hated his juniors proportionately to their youth and health.

And—

" . . . this woman of yours . . . she ain't at home there . . . she ain't at home . . . at home . . . *anywhere* . . . the fat man, the one that kills, he's talking to her but she isn't . . . yes, she is . . . no, she isn't—she's answering him, talking about over-the-sea . . ."

"Lee Falcaro," Charles whispered. "Lee Bennet."

The trance-frozen face didn't change; the eerie whisper went on without interruption: " . . . Lee Bennet on her lips, Lee Falcaro down deep in her guts . . . and the face of Charles Orsino down there too . . ."

An unexpected pang went through him.

On the seventh day they both developed boils, high fever and an enfeebling diarrhea—diet, infection or some animal vector they couldn't cope with. First her perception attenuated as she lay on the grass with dry, hot skin and glazed eyes. Then as she weakened terribly it grew stronger and uncontrollable. The words rushed from her in a torrent, cannoning into each other and making chaos. Much of it Charles did not hear, and much of what he heard he did not remember. He had boils and fever and diarrhea of his own. But some of what he both heard and remembered he tried to forget; it was too terrible a stripping bare, too pitiless a flaying.

Starvation or resistance cured first him and then her. While she recovered and Charles fed her on broth, he sorted and classified endlessly what he had learned. He formed and rejected a dozen plans while Martha's skin-and-bone limbs rounded out again. At last there was one he could not reject.

FIFTEEN

Commander Grinnel was officer of the day, and sore as a boil about it. ONI wasn't supposed to catch the duty. You risked your life on cloak-and-dagger missions; let the shore-bound fancy dans do the drudgery. But there he was, nevertheless, in the guard house office with a .45 on his hip, the interminable night stretching before him, and the ten man main guard snoring away outside. By the book, he should make the rounds of New Portsmouth and check sentries. They would be, however, corked off in storage sheds or notch joints until dawn, at which time they would resume their rounds yawning and waiting to be collected. An over-conscientious junior officer could search them out, shake them awake, bawl hell out of them and go off feeling virtuous. It happened every so often. But he, as a commander, couldn't let it pass without at least special courts for all hands caught sacked up. It would be a hell of a lot of paperwork and bother and it wouldn't look good on his record. The record, the record! You always had to think first and last of the record! *That* was how you made flag rank—that and connections.

He eased his bad military conscience by reflecting that there wasn't anything to guard, that patrolling the shore establishment was just worn-out tradition. The ships and boats had their own watch. At the very furthest stretch of the imagination, a tarzan might sneak into town and try to steal some ammo. Well, if he got caught he got caught. And if he didn't, who'd know the difference with the accounting as sloppy as it was here? They did things differently in Iceland.

He cursed himself for mooning away these hours. It was, after all, a golden opportunity for some hard thinking. You could never think too much about your career. You had to study people out, find their push-buttons, their levers, and decide when to use them.

For instance, he wasn't well enough known to the enlisted men here. They knew vaguely that you couldn't get away with anything when Grinnel was around, but that wasn't enough. His religious study of flag-rank officers showed that they were invariably well known as personalities to the End . . . either for their friendliness and lenience or paradoxically for their aloofness and severity. He, Grinnel, was unfortunately neither one nor the other, and something should be done about it soon. Should he be a good Joe or the roughest son of a bitch in New Portsmouth? He rather thought he'd better be a good Joe. The Guardsmen here were free with their knives. Now he just had to wait for appropriate opportunities.

Grinnel looked at the guardhouse clock, leaned back and beamed. See? A mark of character. Just because you pulled petty routine, it didn't mean the time had to be wasted. You could think things through.

They crept through the midnight dark of New Portsmouth's outskirts. As before, she led with her small hand. Lights flared on a wharf where, perhaps, a boat was being serviced. A slave screamed somewhere under the lash or worse.

"Here's the whorehouse," Martha whispered. It was smack between paydays—part of the plan—and the house was dark except for the hopefully lit parlor. They ducked down the alley that skirted it and around the back of Bachelor Officer Quarters. The sentry, if he were going his rounds at all, would be at the other end of his post when they passed—part of the plan.

Lee Falcaro was quartered alone in a locked room of the ONI building. Marine G-2 and Guard Intelligence School had tried to grab her from ONI, first by requisition and then physically. She conferred prestige on an organization. ONI was protecting the prestige she conferred with a combination lock on her door. Martha had, from seventy miles away, frequently watched the lock being opened and closed.

They dove under the building's crumbling porch two minutes before a late crowd of drinkers roared down the street and emerged when they were safely gone. There was a Charge of Quarters, a little yeoman, snoozing under a dim light in the ONI building's lobby.

"Anybody else?" Charles whispered edgily.

"No. Just her. She's asleep. Dreaming about —never mind. Come on, Charles. He's out."

The little yeoman didn't stir as they passed him and crept up the stairs. Lee Falcaro's room was part of the third-floor attic, finished off specially. You reached it by a ladder from a second-floor one-man office.

The lock was an eight-button piccolo—very rare in New Portsmouth and presumably loot from the mainland. Charles' fingers flew over it: 1-7-5-4, 2-2-7-3, 8-2-6-6—and it flipped open silently.

But the door squeaked.

"She's waking up!" Martha hissed in the dark. "She'll yell!"

Charles reached the bed in two strides and clamped his hand over Lee Falcaro-Bennet's mouth. Only a feeble "mmm!" came out, but the girl thrashed violently in his grip.

"Shut up, lady!" Martha whispered. "No-body's going to rape you."

There was an astonished "mmm?" and she subsided, trembling.

"Go ahead," Martha told him. "She won't yell."

He took his hand away nervously. "We've come to administer the oath of citizenship," he said.

The girl answered in the querulous voice

that was hardly hers: "You picked a strange time for it. Who are you? What's all the whispering for?"

He improvised desperately: "I'm Commander Lister. Just in from Iceland aboard atom sub *Taft*. They didn't tell you in case it got turned down, but I was sent for authorization to give you citizenship. You know how unusual it is for a woman."

"Who's this child? And why did you get me up in the dead of night?"

He dipped deeply into Martha's probings of the past week. "Citizenship'll make the Guard Intelligence gang think twice before they try to grab you again. Naturally they'd try to block us if we administered the oath in public. Ready?"

"Dramatic," she sneered. "Oh, I suppose so. Get it over with."

"Do you, Lee Bennet, solemnly renounce all allegiances previously held by you and pledge your allegiance to the North American Government?"

"I do," she said.

There was a choked little cry from Martha. "Hell's fire," she said. "Like breaking a leg!"

"What are you talking about little girl?" Lee asked, coldly alert.

"It's all right," Charles said wearily. "Don't you know my voice? I'm Orsino. You turned me in back there because they don't give citizenship to women and so your de-conditioning didn't get triggered off. I managed to break for the woods. A bunch of natives got me. I busted loose with the help of Martha here. Among her other talents, the kid's a mind reader. I remember the triggering shocked me out of a year's growth; how do you feel?''

Lee was silent, but Martha answered in a voice half puzzled and half contemptuous: ''She feels fine, but she's crying.''

''—m not,'' Lee Falcaro gulped.

Charles turned from her, embarrassed. In a voice that strove to be normal, he whispered to Martha: ''What about the boat?''

''Still there,'' she said.

Lee Falcaro said tremulously: ''Wh-wh-what boat?''

''Martha's staked out a mini-nuke patrol speedboat at a wharf. One guard aboard. She —watched it in operation and I have some small-boat time. I really think we can grab it. If we get a good head-start, they don't have anything based here that'll catch up with it. If we get a break on the weather, their planes won't be able to pick us up.''

Lee Falcaro stood up, dashing tears from her eyes. ''Then let's go,'' she said evenly.

''How's the CQ—that man downstairs, Martha?''

''Still sleepin'. The way's as clear now as it'll ever be.''

They closed the door behind them and Charles worked the lock. The Charge of Quarters looked as though he couldn't be roused by anything less than an earthquake as they passed—but Martha stumbled on one of the rotting steps after they were outside the building.

"Patrick and Bridget rot my clumsy feet off!" she whispered. "He's awake."

"Under the porch," Charles said. They crawled into the dank space between porch floor and ground. Martha kept up a scarcely audible volleyfire of maledictions aimed at herself.

When they stopped abruptly Charles knew it was bad.

Martha held up her hand for silence, and Charles imagined in the dark that he could see the strained and eerie look of her face. After a pause she whispered: "He's using the—what do you call it? You talk and somebody hears you far away? A prowler, he says to them. A wild man from the woods. The bitch's bastard must have seen you in your handsome suit of skin and dirt, Charles. Oh, we're *for* it! May my toe that stumbled grow the size of a boulder! May my cursed eyes that didn't see the step fall out!"

They huddled down in the darkness and Charles took Lee Falcaro's hand reassuringly. It was cold, and shaken by a fine tremor. A moment later his other hand was taken, with grim possessiveness, by the child.

Martha whispered: "The fat little man. The man who kills, Charles."

He nodded. He thought he had recognized Grinnel from her picture.

"And ten men waking up. Bridget and Patrick rot them! Abaddon stone them! Ah, if only the curses worked on you outlanders we'd be out of here in a wink! Charles, do you remember the way to the wharf?"

"Sure," he said. "But we're not going to get separated. We'll tough this out together."

"They're mean, mad men," she said. "Bloody-minded. And the little man is the worst."

"Sweaters on them?" he asked, thinking of the Guards. "Black clothes that cover their necks?"

"They're the ones."

They heard the stomping feet and a babble of voices, and Commander Grinnel's clear, fat-man's tenor: "Keep it quiet, men. He may still be in the area." The feet thundered over their heads on the porch.

In the barest of whispers Martha said: "The man that slept tells them there was only one, and he didn't see what he was like except for the bare skin and the long hair. And the fat man says they'll find him and—and—and says they'll find him." Her hand clutched Charles' desperately and then dropped it as the feet of the Guardsmen thudded overhead again.

Grinnel was saying: "Half of you head up the street and half down. Check the alleys, check open windows—hell, I don't have to tell you. If we don't find the bastard on the first run we'll have to wake up the whole Guard Battalion and patrol the whole base with them all the goddamn night, so keep your eyes open. Take off."

"Remember the way to the wharf, Charles," Martha said. "Good-by, lady. Take care of him. Take good care of him." She wrenched her hand away and darted out from under the porch.

Lee muttered some agonized monosyllable. Charles started out after the child instinctively and then collapsed weakly back onto the dirt. They heard the rest.

"Hey, you—it's him, by God! Get him! Get him!"

"Here he is, down here! Head him off!"

"Over there!" Grinnel yelled. "Head him off! Head him—good work!"

"For God's sake. It's a girl."

"Those goddamn yeomen and their goddamn prowlers." Grinnel: "Where are you from kid?"

"That's no kid from the base, Commander. Look at her!"

"I just was, sarge. Looks good to me, don't it to you?"

Grinnel, tolerant, fatherly, amused: "Now, men, have your fun but keep it quiet."

"Don't be afraid, kid—" There was an animal howl from Martha's throat that made Lee Falcaro shake hysterically and Charles grind his fingernails into his palms.

"Why, Commander, sometimes I like to make a little noise—"

"Ow!" a man yelled. There was a scuffle of feet and babbling voices. "Get her, you damn fool!" "She bit my hand—" "There she goes—" and a single emphatic shot.

Grinnel's voice said into the silence that followed: "That's that, men."

"Did you *have* to shoot, Commander!" an aggrieved Guardsman said.

"Don't blame me, fellow. Blame the guy that let her go."

"God dammit, she bit me—"

Somebody said as though he didn't mean it: "We ought to take her someplace."

"The hell with that. Let 'em get her in the morning."

"Them as wants her." A cackle of harsh laughter.

Grinnel, tolerantly: "Back to the guardhouse, men. And keep it quiet."

They scuffled off and there was silence again for long minutes. Charles said at last: "We'll go down to the wharf." They crawled out and looked for a moment from the shelter of the building at the bundle lying in the road.

Lee muttered: "Grinnel."

"Shut up," Charles said. He led her down deserted alleys and around empty corners, strictly according to plan.

The speedboat was a twenty-foot craft at Wharf Eighteen, bobbing on the water safely removed from other moored boats and ships. Lee Falcaro let out a small, smothered shriek when she saw a uniformed sailor sitting in the cockpit, apparently staring directly at them.

"It'll be all right," Charles said. "He's a drunkard. He's always out cold by this time of night." Smoothly Charles found the rope locker, cut lengths with the sailor's own knife and bound and gagged him. The man's eyes opened, weary, glazed and red while this was going on, and closed again. "Help me lug him ashore," Charles said. Lee Falcaro took the sailor's legs and they eased him onto the wharf.

They went back into the cockpit. "This is

deep water," Charles said, "so you'll have no
trouble with pilotage. You can read a
compass and charts. There's an automatic
dead reckoner if you want to be fancy. My
advice is just to pull the moderator rods out
quarter-speed, point the thing west, pull the
rods out as far as they'll go—and relax. Either
they'll overtake you or they won't."

She was beginning to get the drift. She said
nervously: "You're talking as though you're
not coming along."

"I'm not," he said, pulling the lock of the
arms rack. The bar fell aside and he pulled a
.45 pistol from its clamp. He thought back and
remembered where the boat's diminutive
magazine was located, broke the feeble lock
and found a box of short, fat heavy little cartridges. He began to snap them into the
pistol's magazine.

"What do you think you're up to?" Lee
Falcaro demanded.

"Appointment with Commander Grinnel,"
he said. He slid the heavy magazine into the
pistol's grip and worked the slide to jack a
cartridge into the chamber.

"Shall I cast off for you?" he asked.

"Don't be a fool," she said. "You can't bring
her back to life and you've got a job to do for
the Syndic."

"You do it," he said, and snapped another of
the blunt, fat little cartridges into the
magazine.

"She's not more important than the
Syndic," Lee Falcaro said.

He hefted the pistol and stuck it into the

belt of his ruined Navy uniform pants. "Yes she is," he said. "Somebody told me once—his name was T. G. Pendleton—that you can only be loyal to people. The Syndic is people. It's got a lot of friends. We don't have the exact dope we were sent to get, but we do have some useful stuff for them. If you don't get through, they'll find others who will. But the kid didn't have anybody but me. Her own sister—it's too long to explain and it'd only sound funny. What the hell difference does it make if I never play another chukker of polo again? But it makes a big, big difference if I let Grinnel get away with what he did. He could have stopped those apes, but he didn't. I can stop Grinnel—maybe. If I don't choose to, I'm as low as he is."

She was slowly filling the magazine of another .45 from the arms rack. "Don't cast off for a couple of minutes," he said. "The boat's noisy and it'll bring a crowd. They won't get organized enough to take off after you for a while, but I'm conspicuous. Good-by."

He made ready to step from the cockpit to the wharf.

"Wait," she said slowly. "Is this thing ready to fire?"

She passed him the pistol. He worked the slide, snapping a cartridge into the chamber, and thumbed down the safety. Somewhere a woman was laughing a shrill, drunken laugh. Somewhere a big lathe or drill was biting into stubborn metal with a squealing, tortured noise. Charles handed back the .45 and said:

"You just point it and pull the trigger."

Lee Falcaro pointed the pistol unsteadily at his middle. "You're coming with me," she said. "If you won't listen to reason, I'll put a bullet in your leg." Shock held him while she groped one-handed, for the moderator-rod control and pulled it hard.

"Christ," he gasped, "you'll sink us!" and dashed for the controls. You had seconds before the wormgears turned, the cadmium rods withdrew from their slots, the reactor seethed and sent boiling metal cycling through the turbine—

He slammed down manual levers that threw off the fore and aft mooring lines, spun the wheel, bracing himself, and saw Lee Falcaro go down to the deck in a tangle, the .45 flying from her hand and skidding across the knurled plastic planking. But by then the turbine was screaming an alarm to the whole base and they were cutting white water through the buoy-marked gap in the harbor net.

Lee Falcaro got to her feet. "I'm not proud of myself," she said to him, "but she told me to take care of you."

He said grimly: "We could have gone straight to the wharf without that little lay-over to pick you up. Take the wheel."

"Charles, I—"

"Take the wheel."

She did, and he went aft to stare through the darkness. The harbor lights were twinkling pinpoints; then his eyes misted so he could not see them at all. He didn't give a damn if a dozen corvettes were already slicing the bay in pursuit. He had failed miserably at the only important job that had ever come his way. And worse, he knew he had wanted to fail.

SIXTEEN

It was a dank fog-shrouded morning. Sometime during the night the quill of the dead reckoner had traced its fine red line over the 30th meridian. Roughly halfway, Charles Orsino thought, rubbing the sleep from his eyes. But the line was straight as a string for the last four hours of their run. The damn girl must have fallen asleep on watch. He glared at her in the bow and broke open a ration. Blandly oblivious to the glare, she said: "Good morning."

Charles swallowed a mouthful of chocolate, half-chewed, and choked on it. He reached hastily for water and found the tall plastic column of the ion-exchange apparatus empty. "Damn it," he snarled, "why didn't you refill this thing when you emptied it? And why didn't you zigzag overnight? You're utterly irresponsible." He hurled the bucket overside, hauled it up and slopped sea water into the apparatus. Now there'd be a good twenty minutes before a man-sized drink accumulated, he growled to himself.

"Just a minute," she told him steadily. "Let's straighten this out. I haven't had any water on the night watch so I didn't have any occasion to refill the tube. You must have taken the last of the water with your dinner. And as for the zigzag, you said we should run a straightaway now and then to mix it up. I decided that last night was as good a time as any." She watched him, waiting.

He took a minute drink from the reservoir, stalling. There was something—yes; he had *meant* to refill the apparatus after his dinner ration. And he *had* told her to give it a few hours of straightaway some night . . . .

He said formally: "You're quite right on both counts. I apologize." He bit into something that tasted like a cake of peanut butter compacted under enormous hydraulic pressure.

"That's not good enough," she said. "I'm not going to have you tell me you're sorry and then go scowling and sulking about the boat. In fact I don't like your behavior at all."

He said, enormously angry: "*Oh, you don't do you?*" and hating her, the world and himself for the stupid inadequacy of the comeback, crudely and vulgarly spat the nauseating mouthful overside.

"No. I don't. I'm seriously worried. I'm afraid the conditioning you got didn't fall away completely when they swore you in. You've been acting irrationally and inconsistently."

"What about you?" he snapped. "You got conditioned too."

"That's right," she said. "That's another reason why you're worrying me. I find impulses in myself that have no business there. I simply seem to do a better job of controlling them than you're doing. For instance: we've been quarreling and at cross-purposes ever since you and Martha picked me up. That couldn't be unless I were contributing to the friction."

The wheel was fixed; she took a step or two aft and said professorially: "I've never had trouble getting along with people. I've had differences, of course, and at times I've allowed myself displays of temper when it was necessary to assert myself. But I find that you upset me; that for some reason or other your opinion on a matter is important to me, that if it differs with mine there should be a reconciliation."

He put down the ration and said wonderingly: "Do you know, that's the way I feel about you? And you think it's the conditioning or—or something?" He took a couple of steps forward, hesitantly.

"Yes," she said in a rather tremulous voice. "The conditioning or something. For instance, you're inhibited. You haven't made an indecent proposition to me, not even as a matter of courtesy. Not that I care, of course, but—" In stepping aft, she tripped over the water bucket and went down to the deck with a faint scream.

He said: "Here, let me help you." He picked

her up and didn't let go.

"Thanks," she said faintly. "The conditioning technique can't be called faulty, but it has inherent limitations . . ." She trailed off and he kissed her. She kissed back and said more faintly still: "Or it might be the drugs we used . . . Oh, Charles, what *took* you so long?"

"I don't know," he said, brooding. "You're way out of my class, you know. I'm just a bagman for the New York Police. I wouldn't even be that if it weren't for Uncle Frank, and you're a Falcaro. It's just barely thinkable that I could make a pass at you. I guess that held me off and I didn't want to admit it so I got mad at you instead. Hell. I could have swum back to the base and made a damned fool of myself trying to find Grinnel, but down inside I knew better. The kid's *gone*."

"We'll make a psychologist of you yet," she said.

"Psychologist? Why, you're joking."

"No. It's not a joke. You'll *like* psychology, darling. You can't go on playing polo forever, you know."

Darling! What was he getting into? Old man Gilby was four-goal at sixty, wasn't he? Good God, was he hooked into marriage at twenty-three? Was she married already? Did she know or care whether he was? Had she been promiscuous? Would she continue to be? What went on here? Let me out! It went through his mind in a single panicky flash and then he said: "The hell with it," and kissed her again.

She wanted to know: "The hell with what, darling?"

"Everything. Tell me about psychology. I can't go on playing polo forever."

It was an hour before she got around to telling him about psychology: "The neglect has been criminal—and inexplicable. For about a century it's been *assumed* that psychology is a dead fallacy. Why?"

"All right," he said amiably, playing with a lock of her hair. "Why?"

"Lieberman," she said. "Lieberman of Johns Hopkins. He was one of the old-line topological psychology men—don't let the lingo throw you, Charles; it's just the name of a system. He wrote the hell of an attack on the *mengenlehre* psychology school—point-sets of emotions, class-inclusions of reactions and so on. He blasted them to bits by proving that their constructs didn't correspond to the emotions and reactions of random-sampled populations. And then came the payoff: he tried the same acid test on his *own* school's constructs and found out that they didn't correspond either. It didn't frighten him; he was a scientist. He published, and then the jig was up. Everybody, from full professors to undergraduate students went down the roster of the schools of psychology and wrecked them so comprehensively that the field was as dead as palmistry in twenty years. The miracle is that it hadn't happened before. The flaws were so glaring! Textbooks of the older kind solemnly described syndromes, psychoses, neuroses that simply couldn't be found in the real world! And that's the way it was all the way down the line."

"So where does that leave us?" Charles demanded. "Is it is or is it ain't a science?"

"It is," she said simply. "Lieberman and his followers went too far. It became a kind of hysteria. The experimenters must have been too eager. They misread results, they misinterpreted statistics, they misunderstood the claims of a school and knocked down not its true claims but strawman claims they had set up themselves."

"But — *psychology*!" Charles protested, obscurely embarrassed at the thought that man's mind was subject to scientific study— not because he knew the first thing about it, but because *everybody* knew psychology was phony.

She shrugged. "I can't help it. We were doing physiology of the sensory organs, trying to settle the oldie about focusing the eye, and I got to grubbing around the pre-Lieberman texts looking for light in the darkness. Some of it sounded so—not sensible, but *positive* that I ran off one of Lieberman's population checks. And the old boy had been dead wrong. *Mengenlehre* constructs correspond quite nicely to the actual way people's minds work. I kept checking and the schools that were destroyed as hopelessly fallacious a century ago checked out, some closely and some not so closely, as good descriptions of the way the mind works. Some have predictive value. I used *mengenlehre* psychology algorisms to compute the conditioning on you and me, in-

cluding the trigger release. It worked. You
see, Charles? We're on the rim of something
tremendous!"

"When did this Lieberman flourish?"

"I don't have the exact dates in my head.
The breakup of the schools corresponded
roughly with the lifetime of John G. Falcaro."

That pinpointed it rather well. John G. succeeded Rafael, who succeeded Amadeo
Falcaro, first leader of the Syndic in revolt.
Under John G., the hard-won freedom was enjoyed, the bulging storehouses were joyously emptied, craft union rules went joyously out the window and builders *worked*,
the dollar faded away but the carlo bought
plenty and there was a large number of carlos
in circulation. It had been an exuberant time
still fondly remembered; just the time for
over-enthusiastic rebels against a fusty schol-
asticism to joyously smash old ways of
thought without too much exercise of the conscience. It all checked out.

He started and got to his feet. A hardly
noticed discomfort was becoming acute; the
speedboat was pitching and rolling quite
seriously, for the first time since their escape.
"Dirty weather coming up," he said. "We've
been too damned lucky so far." He thought,
but didn't remark, that there was much to
worry about in the fact that there seemed to
have been no pursuit. The meager resources
of the North American Navy wouldn't be
spent on chasing a single minor craft—not if
the weather could be counted on to finish her
off.

"I thought we were unsinkable?"

"In a way. Seal the boat and she's unsinkable the way a corked bottle is. But the boat's made up of a lot of bits and pieces that go together just so. Pound her for a few hours with waves and the bits and pieces give way. She doesn't sink, but she doesn't steam or steer either. I wish the Syndic had a fleet on the Atlantic."

"There's nothing on the Atlantic," she said positively.

The sea-search radar pinged and they flew to the screen. "*Something* at 273 degrees, about eight miles," he said. "It can't be pursuit. They couldn't have any reason at all to circle around us and come at us from ahead." He strained his eyes into the west and thought he could see a black speck on the gray.

Lee Falcaro tried a pair of binoculars and complained: "These things won't work."

"Not on a rolling, pitching platform they won't—not with an optical lever eight miles long. There was something about a gyro-stabilized signal glass, but I don't suppose this boat would have one." He spun the wheel to 180; they staggered and clung on as the bow whipped about, searched and steadied on the new course. The mounting waves slammed them broadside-to and the rolling increased. They hardly noticed; their eyes were on the radarscope. Fogged as it was with sea return, they nevertheless could be sure after several minutes that the object had changed course to 135. Charles made a flying guess at her speed, read their own speed off and scribbled for a moment.

He said nothing, but spun the wheel to 225

and went back to the radarscope. The object changed course to 145. Charles scribbled again and said at last, flatly: "They're running collision courses on us. Automatically computed. I suppose, from a radar. We're through."

"We *can't* be," the girl said incredulously. "We're faster."

"Doesn't matter." He spun the wheel to 180 again, and studied the crawling green spark on the radarscope. "This way we give 'em the longest run for their money and can pray for a miracle. The only way we can use our speed to outrun them is to turn around and head back into Government Territory—which isn't what we want. Relax and pray, Lee. Maybe if the weather thickens they'll lose us—no; not with radar."

They sat together on a bunk, wordlessly, for hours while the spray dashed higher and the boat shivered to hammering waves. Briefly they saw the pursuer, three miles off, low, black and ugly, before fog closed in again.

At nightfall there was the close, triumphant roar of a big reaction turbine and a light stabbed through the fog, flooding the boat with blue-white radiance. A cliff-like black hull loomed alongside as a bullhorn roared at them: "Cut your engines and come about into the wind."

Lee Falcaro read white-painted letters on the black hull; "*Hon. James J. Regan,* Chicago." She turned to Charles and said wonderingly: "It's an ore boat. From the Mob Great Lakes fleet."

SEVENTEEN

"Here?" Charles demanded. *"Here?"*

"No possible mistake," she said, stunned. "When you're a Falcaro you travel. I've seen 'em in Duluth, I've seen 'em in Quebec, I've seen 'em in Buffalo."

The bull-horn voice roared again, dead in the shroud of fog: "Come into the wind and cut your engines or we'll put a shell into you."

Charles turned the wheel and wound in the moderator rod; the boat pitched like a splinter on the waves. There was a muffled double explosion and two grapnels crunched into the plastic hull, bow and stern. As the boat steadied, sharing the inertia of the ore ship, a dark figure leaped from the blue-white eye of the searchlight to their deck. And another. And another.

"Hello, Jim," Lee Falcaro said almost inaudibly. "Haven't met since Las Vegas, have we?"

The first boarder studied her coolly. He was built for football or any other form of mayhem . . . . He ignored Charles completely. "Lee Falcaro is advised. Do you still think twenty reds means a black is bound to come up? You always were a fool, Lee. And now you're in real trouble."

"What's going on, mister?" Charles snapped. "We're Syndics and I presume you're Mobsters. Don't you recognize the Treaty?"

The boarder turned to Charles inquiringly. "Some confusion," he said. "Max Wyman? Charles Orsino? Or just some wildman from outback?"

"Orsino," Charles said formally. "Second cousin of Edward Falcaro, under the guardianship of Francis W. Taylor."

The boarder bowed slightly. "James Regan IV," he said. "No need to list my connections. It would take too long and I feel no need to justify myself to a small-time Dago chiseler. Watch him, gentlemen!"

Charles found his arms pinned by Regan's two companions. There was a gun muzzle in his ribs.

Regan shouted to the ship and a ladder was let down. Lee Falcaro and Charles climbed it with guns at their backs. He said to her: "Who is that lunatic?" It did not even occur to him that the young man was who he claimed to be —the son of the Mob Territory opposite number of Edward Falcaro.

"He's Regan," she said. "And I don't know who's the lunatic, him or me. Charles, I'm sorry, terribly sorry, I got you into this."

He managed to smile. "I volunteered," he said.

"Enough talk," Regan said, following them onto the deck. Dull-eyed sailors watched them incuriously, and there were a couple of anvil-jawed men with a stance and swagger Charles had come to know. Guardsmen—he would have staked his life on it. Guardsmen of the North American Government Navy—aboard a Mob Territory ship and acting as if they were passengers or high-rated crewmen.

Regan smirked: "I'm on the horns of a dilemma. There are no accommodations that are quite right for you. There are storage compartments which are worse than you deserve and there are passenger quarters which are too good for you. I'm afraid it will have to be one of the compartments. Your consolation will be that it's only a short run to Chicago."

Chicago—headquarters for Mob Territory. The ore ship had been on a return trip to Chicago when alerted somehow by the Navy to intercept the fugitives. *Why?*

"Down there," one of the men gestured briskly with a gun. They climbed down a ladder into a dark, oily cavern fitfully lit by a flash in Regan's hand.

"Make yourselves comfortable," Regan told them. "If you get a headache, don't worry. We were carrying some avgas on the outward run." The flash winked out and a door clanged on them.

"I can't believe it," Charles said. "That's a top Mob man? Couldn't you be mistaken?" He groped in the dark and found her. The place did reek of gasoline.

She clung to him and said: "Hold me, Charles . . . . Yes that's Jimmy Regan. That's what will become top man in the Mob. Jimmy's a charmer at a Las Vegas hotel. Jimmy's a gourmet when he orders at the Pump Room and he's trying to overawe you. He ordered kebabs on a flaming sword. I ordered scrambled eggs flambée served on a saber and he never knew I was kidding. Jimmy plays polo too, but he's crippled three of his own teammates because he's not very good at it. I kept telling myself whenever I ran into him that he was just an accident, the Mob could survive him. But his father acts—funny. There's something wrong with them; there's something wrong with the Mob. They roll out the carpet when you show up but the people around them are afraid of them. There's a story I never believed—but I believe it now. What would happen if my uncle pulled out a pistol and began screaming and shot a waiter? Jimmy's father did it, they tell me. And nothing happened except that the waiter was dragged away and everybody said it was a good thing Mr. Regan saw him reach for his gun and shot him first. Only the waiter didn't have any gun. I saw Jimmy last three years ago. I haven't been in Mob Territory since. I didn't like it there. Now I know why. Give Mob Territory enough time and it'll be like New Portsmouth. Something went wrong with them. We have the Treaty of Las Vegas and a hundred years of peace and there aren't

many people going back and forth between
Syndic and Mob except for a few high-ups like
me who have to circulate. Manners. So you
pay duty calls and shut your eyes to what
they're really like.

"*This* is what they're like. This dark, damp
stinking compartment. And my uncle—and all
the Falcaros—and you—and I—we're like
sunlit fields compared to them. Aren't we?
Aren't we?" Her fingers bit into his arms.

"Easy," he soothed her. "Easy, easy. We're
all right. We'll be all right. I think I've got it
figured out. This must be some private gun-
running Jimmy's gone in for. Loaded an ore
boat with avgas and ammo and ran it up the
Seaway. If anybody in Syndic Territory gave a
damn they thought it was a load of ore for
New Orleans via the Atlantic and the Gulf. But
Jimmy ran his load to Ireland or Iceland HQ.
A little private flier of his. He wouldn't dare
harm us. There's the Treaty and you're a Falcaro."

"Treaty," she said. "I tell you they're all in
it. Now that I've seen the Government in action I understand what I saw in Mob Territory. They've gone rotten, that's all. They've
gone rotten. The way he treated you, because
he thought you didn't have his rank! Sometimes my uncle's high-handed, sometimes he
tells a person off, sometimes he lets him know
he's top man in the Syndic and doesn't propose to let anybody teach him how to suck
eggs. But the spirit's different. In the Syndic
it's parent to child. In the Mob it's master to
slave. Not based on age, not based on achieve-

ment, but based on the accident of birth. You tell me 'You're a Falcaro' and that packs weight. Why? Not because I was born a Falcaro but because they let me stay a Falcaro. If I hadn't been brainy and quick, they'd have adopted me out before I was ten. They don't do that in Mob Territory. Whatever chance sends, a Regan is a Regan then and forever. Even if it's a paranoid constitutional inferior like Jimmy's father. Even if it's a giggling pervert like Jimmy.

"God, Charles, I'm scared.

"At last I know these people and I'm scared. You'd have to see Chicago to know why. The lakefront palaces, finer than anything in New York. Regan Memorial Plaza, finer than Scratch Sheet Square—great gilded marble figures, a hundred running yards of heroic frieze. But the hovels you see only by chance! Gray brick towers dating from the Third Fire! The children with faces like weasels, the men with faces like hogs, the women with figures like beer barrels and all of them glaring at you when you drive past as if they could cut your throat with joy. I never understood the look in their eyes until now, and you'll never begin to understand what I'm talking about until you see their eyes . . . ."

Charles revolted against the idea. It was too gross to go down. It didn't square with his acquired picture of life in North America and therefore Lee Falcaro must be somehow mistaken or hysterical. "There," he murmured, stroking her hair. "We'll be all right. We'll be all right."

She twisted out of his arms and raged: "I *won't* be humored. They're mad, I tell you. Dick Reiner was right. We've got to wipe out the Government. But Frank Taylor was right too. We've got to blast the Mob before they blast us. They've died and decayed into something too horrible to bear. If we let them stay on the Continent with us their stink will infect us and poison us to death. We've got to do something. We've got to do something."

"What?"

It stopped her cold. After a minute she uttered a shaky laugh. "The fat, sloppy, happy Syndic," she said, "sitting around while the wolves overseas and the maniacs across the Mississippi are waiting to jump. Yes—do what?"

Charles Orsino was not good at arguments, or indeed at any abstract thinking. He knew it. He knew the virtues that had commended him to F. W. Taylor were his energy and an off-hand talent for getting along with people. But something on the abstract level rang terribly false in Lee's words.

"That kind of thinking doesn't get you anywhere, Lee," he said slowly. "I didn't absorb much from Uncle Frank, but I did absorb this: you run into trouble if you make up stories about the world and then act as if they're true. The Syndic isn't somebody sitting around. The Government isn't wolves. The Mobsters aren't maniacs. And they aren't waiting to jump on the Syndic. The Syndic isn't anything that's jumpable. It's some people and their morale and credit."

"Faith is a beautiful thing," Lee Falcaro said bitterly. "Where'd you get yours?"

"From the people I knew and worked with. Bartenders, bookies, cops. Decent citizens."

"And what about the scared and unhappy ones in Riveredge? That sow of a woman in the D.A.R. who smuggled me aboard a coast raider? The neurotics and psychotics I found more and more of when I invalidated the Lieberman findings? Charles, the North American Government didn't scare me especially. But the thought that they're lined up with a continental power does. It scares me damnably because it'll be three against one. Against the Syndic, the Mob, the Government —and our own unbalanced citizens."

Uncle Frank never let that word "citizens" pass without a tirade. "We are not a government!" he always yelled. "We are not a government! We must not think like a government! We must not think in terms of duties and receipts and disbursements. We must think in terms of the old loyalties that bound the Syndic together!" Uncle Frank was sedentary, but he had roused himself once to the point of wrecking a bright young man's newly installed record keeping system for the Medical Center. He had used a cane, most enthusiastically, and then bellowed: "The next wise guy who tries to sneak systems analysis into this joint will get it down his throat! What the hell do we need systems analysis for? Either there's room enough and doctors enough for the patients or there isn't. If there is, we take care of them. If there isn't, we put'em in an ambulance and take them some-place else. And if I hear one God-damned word about 'efficiency'—" He glared the rest and strode out, puffing and leaning on Charles' arm. "Efficiency," he growled in the corridor. "Every so often a wise guy comes to me whimpering that people are getting away with murder, collections are ten per cent below what they ought to be, the Falcaro Fund's being milked because fifteen per cent of the dough goes to people who aren't in need at all, eight per cent of the people getting old-age pensions aren't really past sixty. Get efficient, these people tell me. Save money by triple-checking collections. Save money by tightening up the Fund rules. Save money by a nice big vital-statistics system so we can check on pensioners. Yeah! Have people who might be *working* check on collections instead, and make enemies to boot whenever we catch somebody short. Make the Fund a grudging Scrooge instead of an open-handed sugar-daddy—and let people *worry* about their chances of making the Fund instead of *knowing* it'll take care of them if they're caught short. Set up a vital statistics system from birth to death, with numbers and fingerprints and house registration and maybe the gas chamber if you forget to report a brother-in-law moving in. You know what's wrong with the wise guys, Charles? Constipation. And they want to constipate the universe." Charles remembered his uncle restored to chuckling good humor by the time he had finished em-broidering his spur-of-the-moment theory with elaborate scatological details.

"The Syndic will stand," he said to Lee Falcaro, thinking of his uncle who knew what he was doing, thinking of Edward Falcaro who did the right thing without knowing why, thinking of his good friends in the 101st Precinct, the roaring happy crowds in Scratch Sheet Square, the good-hearted men of Riveredge Breakdown Station 26 who had borne with his sullenness and intolerance simply because that was the way things were and that was the way you acted. "I don't know what the Mob's up to, and I got a shock from the Government, and I don't deny that we have a few miserable people who can't seem to be helped. But you've seen too much of the Mob and Government and our abnormals. Maybe you don't know as much as you should about our ordinary people. Anyway, all we can do is wait."

"Yes," she said. "All we can do is wait. Until Chicago we have each other."

EIGHTEEN

They were too sick with gasoline fumes to count the passing hours or days. Food was brought to them from time to time, but it tasted like avgas. They could not think for the sick headaches that pounded incessantly behind their eyes. When Lee developed vomiting spasms that would not stop, Charles Orsino pounded on the bulkhead with his fists and yelled, his voice thunderous in the metal compartment, for an hour.

Somebody came at last—Regan. The light stabbed Charles' eyes when he opened the door. "Trouble?" Regan asked, smirking.

"Miss Falcaro may be dying," Charles said. His own throat felt as though it had been gone over with a cobbler's rasp. "I don't have to tell you your life won't be worth a dime if she dies and it gets back to Syndic Territory. She's got to be moved and she's got to have medical attention."

"Death threat from the Dago?" Regan was amused. "I have it on your own testimony that the Syndic is merely morale and people and credit—not a formidable organization. Yes, there was a bug in here. One reason for your discomfort. You'll be gratified to learn that I thought most of your conversation decidedly dull. However, the lady will be of no use to us dead and we're now in the Seaway entering Lake Michigan. I suppose it can't do any harm to move you two. Pick her up, will you? I'll let you lead the way—and I'll remind you that I may not, as the lady said, be a four-goal polo player but I am a high expert with the handgun. Get moving."

Charles did not think he could pick his own feet up, but pleading weakness to Regan was unbearable. He could try. Staggering, he got Lee Falcaro over his shoulder and through the door. Regan courteously stood aside and murmured: "Straight ahead and up the ramp. I'm giving you my own cabin. We'll be docking soon enough; I'll make out."

Charles dropped her onto a sybaritic bed in a small but lavishly appointed cabin. Regan whistled up a deckhand and ship's officer of some sort, who arrived with a medicine chest. "Do what you can for her, mister," he told the officer. And to the deckhand: "Just watch them. They aren't to touch anything. If they give you trouble, you're free to punch them around a bit." He left, whistling.

The officer fussed unhappily over the medicine chest and stalled by sponging off Lee Falcaro's face and throat. The deckhand watched impassively. He was a six-footer, and he hadn't spent days inhaling casing-head fumes. The triphammer pounding behind Charles' eyes seemed to be worsening with the fresher air. He collapsed into a seat and croaked, with shut eyes: "While you're trying to figure out the vomiting, can I have a handful of aspirins?"

"Eh? Nothing was said about you. You were in Number Three with her? I suppose it'll be all right. Here." He poured a dozen tablets into Charles' hand. "Get him some water, you." The deckhand brought a glass of water from the adjoining lavatory and Charles washed down some of the tablets. The officer was reading a booklet by then, worry on his face. "Do you know any medicine?" he finally asked.

The hard-outlined, kidney-shaped ache was beginning to diffuse through Charles' head, more general now and less excruciating. He felt deliciously sleepy, but roused himself to answer: "Some athletic trainer stuff. I don't know—morphine? Curare?"

The officer ruffled through the booklet. "Nothing about vomiting," he said. "But it says curare for muscular cramp and I guess that's what's going on. A lipoid suspension to release it slowly into the bloodstream and give the irritation time to subside. Anyway, I can't kill her if I watch the dose . . . ."

Charles, through half-opened eyes, saw Lee Falcaro's arm reach behind the officer's back to his medicine chest. The deckhand's eyes were turning to the bed—Charles heaved himself to his feet, skyrockets going off again through his head, and started for the lavatory. The deckhand grabbed his arm. "Rest, mister. Where do you think you're going?"

"Another glass of water—"

"*I'll* get it. You heard my orders."

Charles subsided. When he dared to look again, Lee's arm lay alongside her body and the officer was triple-checking dosages in his booklet against a pressurized hypodermic spray. The officer sighed and addressed Lee: "You won't even feel this. Relax." He read his setting on the spray again, checked it again against the booklet. He touched the syringe to the skin of Lee's arm and thumbed open the valve. It hissed for a moment and Charles knew submicroscopic particles of the medication had been blasted under Lee's skin too fast for nerves to register the shock.

His glass of water came and he gulped it greedily. The officer packed the pressurized syringe away, folded the chest and said to both of them, rather vaguely: "That should do it. If, uh, if anything happens—or if it doesn't work—call me and I'll try something else. Morphine, maybe."

He left and Charles slumped in the chair, the pain ebbing and sleep beginning to flow over him. Not yet, he told himself. She hooked something from the chest. He said to the deckhand: "Can I clean the lady and myself up?"

"Go ahead, mister. You can use it. Just don't try anything."

The man lounged in the doorframe of the lavatory alternately studying Charles at the washbasin and Lee on the bed. Charles took off a heavy layer of oily grease from himself and then took washing tissues to the bed. Lee Falcaro's spasms were tapering off. As he washed her, she managed a smile and an unmistakable wink.

"You folks married?" the deckhand asked.

"No," Charles said. Weakly she held up her right arm for the washing tissue. As he scrubbed the hand, he felt a small cylinder smoothly transferred from her palm to his. He slid it into a pocket and finished the job.

The officer popped in again with a carton of milk.

"Any better, Miss?" he asked.

"Yes," she whispered.

"Good. Try to drink this." Immensely set up by his success in treatment, he hovered over her for a quarter of an hour getting the milk down a sip at a time. It stayed down. He left trailing a favorable prognosis. Meanwhile, Charles had covertly examined Lee's booty: a pressurized syringe labeled "morphine sulfate sol." It was full and ready. He cracked off the protective cap and waited his chance.

It came when Lee grimaced at him and called the deckhand in a feeble murmur. She continued to murmur so indistinctly that he bent over trying to catch the words. Charles leaned forward and emptied the syringe at one-inch range into the taut seat of the deckhand's pants. He scratched absently and said to Lee: "You'll have to talk up, lady." Then he giggled, looked bewildered and collapsed on the floor, staring, coked to the eyebrows.

Lee painfully sat up on the bed. "Porthole," she said.

Charles went to it and struggled with the locking lugs. It opened—and an alarm bell began to clang through the ship. *Now* he saw the hair-fine, broken wire.

Feet thundered outside and the glutinous voice of Jimmy Regan was heard: "Wait, you damn fools! You in there—is everything all right? Did they try to pull something?"

Charles kept silent and shook his head at the girl. He picked up a chair and stood by the door. The glutinous voice again, in a mumble that didn't carry through—and the door sprang open. Charles brought the chair down in a murderous chop, conscious only that it seemed curiously light.

It was Regan, with a drawn gun. It had been Regan. His skull was smashed before he knew it. Charles felt as though he had all the time in the world. He picked up the gun to a confused roar like a slowed-down sound track and emptied it into the corridor. It had been a full automatic, but the fifteen shots seemed as well-spaced as a ceremonial salute. Regan, in his vanity, wore two guns. Charles scooped up the other and said to Lee: "Come on."

He knew she was following as he raced down the cleared corridor and down the ramp, back to the compartment in which they had been locked. Red danger lights burned on the walls. Charles flipped the pistol to semi-automatic as they passed a red-painted bulkhead with valves and gauges sprouting from it. He turned and fired three deliberate shots into it. The last was drowned out by a dull roar as gasoline fumes exploded. Pipe fittings and fragments of plate whizzed about them like bullets as they raced on.

Somebody ahead loomed, yelling querulously: "What the hell was that, Mac? What blew?"

"Where's the reactor room?" Charles demanded, jamming the pistol into his chest. The man gulped and pointed.

"Take me there. Fast."

"Now *look*, Mac—"

Charles told him in a few incisive details where and how he was going to be shot. The man went white and led them down the corridor and into the reactor room. Three white-coated men with the aloof look of reactor specialists stared at them as they bulled into the spotless chamber.

The oldest sniffed: "And what, may I ask, are you crewmen doing in—"

Lee slammed the door behind them and said: "Sound the radiation alarm."

"Certainly not! You must be the couple we—"

"Sound the radiation alarm." She picked up a pair of dividers from the plot board and approached the technician with murder on her face. He gaped until she poised the needle points before his eyes and repeated: *"Sound the radiation alarm."* Nobody in the room, including Charles, had the slightest doubt that the points would sink into the technician's eyeballs if he refused.

"Do what she says, Will," he mumbled, his eyes crossing on the dividers. "For God's sake, do what she says. She's crazy."

One of the men moved, very cautiously, watching Charles and the gun, to a red handle and pulled it down. A ferro-concrete barrier rose to wall off the chamber and the sine-curve wail of a standard radioactivity warning began to howl mournfully through the ship.

"Dump the reactor metal," Charles said. His eyes searched for the exit, and found it —a red-painted breakaway panel, standard for a hot lab.

A technician wailed: "We *can't* do that! We can't *do* that! A million alphs of nuclides with a hundred years of life in them—have a heart, mister! They'll crucify us!"

"They can dredge for it," Charles said. "Dump the metal."

"Dump the metal," Lee said. She hadn't moved.

The senior technician's eyes were still on the bright needle points. He was crying silently. "Dump it," he said.

"Okay, chief. Your responsibility, remember."

"Dump it!" wailed the senior.

The technician did something technical at the control board. After a moment the steady rumbling of the turbines ceased and the ship's deck began to wallow underfoot.

"Hit the panel, Lee," Charles said. She did, running. He followed her through the oval port. It was like an open-bottomed diving bell welded to the hull. There were large, luminous cleats for pulling yourself down through the water, under the rim of the bell. He dropped the pistol into the water, breathed deeply a couple of times and began to climb down. There was no sign of Lee.

He kicked up through the dark water on a long slant away from the ship. It might be worse. With a fire and a hot-lab alarm and a dead chief aboard, the crew would have things on their mind besides looking for bobbing heads.

He broke the surface and treaded water to make a minimum target. He did not turn to the ship. His dark hair would be less visible than his white face. And if he was going to get a burst of machine-gun bullets through either, he didn't want to know about it. Ahead he saw Lee's blond hair spread on the water for a moment and then it vanished. He breathed hugely, dived and swam under water toward it.

When he rose next a sheet of flames was lighting the sky and the oily reek of burning hydrocarbons tainted the air. He dove again, and this time caught up with Lee. Her face was bone-white and her eyes blank. Where she was drawing her strength from he could not guess. Behind them the ship sent up an oily plume and the sine-curve wail of the radioactivity warning could be faintly heard. Before them a dim shore stretched.

He gripped her naked arm, roughened by the March waters of Lake Michigan, bent it around his neck and struck off for the shore. His lungs were bursting in his chest and the world was turning gray-black before his burning eyes. He heaved his tired arm through the water as though each stroke would be his last, but the last stroke, by some miracle, never was the last.

NINETEEN

It hadn't been easy to get time off from the oil-painting factory. Ken Oliver was a little late when he slid into the aseptic-smelling waiting room of the Michigan City Medical Center. A parabolic mike in the ceiling trained itself on the heat he radiated and followed him across the floor to a chair. A canned voice said: "State your business, please."

He started a little and said in the general direction of the mike: "I'm Ken Oliver. A figure man in the Blue Department, Picasso Oils and Etchings Corporation. Dr. Latham sent me here for—what do you call it?—a biopsy."

"Thank you, please be seated."

He smiled because he was seated already and picked up a magazine, the current copy of the *Illinois Sporting News*, familiarly known as the Green Sheet. Everybody in Mob Territory read it. The fingers of the blind spelled out its optimism and its selections at Hawthorne in Braille. If you were not only blind but fingerless, there was a talking edition that read itself aloud to you.

He riffled through the past performances and selections to the articles. This month's lead was—"Thank God I am Dying of Throat Cancer."

He leaned back in the chair dizzily, the waiting room becoming gray mist around him. *No*, he thought. *No*. It couldn't be that. All it could be was a little sore on the back of his throat—no more than that. Just a little sore on the back of his throat. He'd been a fool to go to Latham. The fees were outrageous and he was behind, always a little behind, on his bills. But cancer—so much of it around—and the drugs didn't seem to *help* any more . . . . But Latham had almost promised him it was non-malignant.

"Mr. Oliver," the loudspeaker said, "please go to Dr. Riordan's office, Number Ten."

Riordan was younger than he. That was supposed to be bad in a general practitioner, good in a specialist. And Riordan was a specialist—pathology. A sour-faced young specialist.

"Good morning. Sit here. Open your mouth. Wider than that, and relax. *Relax*; your glottis is locked."

Oliver couldn't protest around the plastic-and-alcohol taste of the tongue depressor. There was a sudden coldness and a metallic *snick* that startled him greatly; then Riordan took the splint out of his mouth and ignored

him as he summoned somebody over his desk
set. A young man, even younger than Riordan,
came in. "Freeze, section and stain this right
away," the pathologist said, handing him a
forceps from which a small blob dangled.
"Have them send up the Rotino charts, three
hundred to nine hundred inclusive."

He began to fill out charts, still ignoring
Oliver, who sat and sweated bullets for ten
minutes. Then he left and was back in five
minutes more.

"You've got it," he said shortly. "It's operable and you won't lose much tissue." He
scribbled on a sheet of paper and handed it to
Oliver. The painter numbly read: " . . . anter-
ior . . . epithelioma . . . metastases . . . giant
cells . . ."

Riordan was talking again: "Give this to
Latham. It's my report. Have him line up a
surgeon. As to the operation, I say the sooner
the better unless you care to lose your larynx.
That will be fifty alphs."

"Fifty alphs," the painter said blankly. "But
Dr. Latham told me—" He trailed off and got
out his checkbook. Only thirty-two in the ac-
count, but he would deposit his paycheck today, which would bring it up. It was after
three so his check wouldn't go in today—he
wrote out the slip slowly and carefully.

Riordan took it, read it suspiciously, put it
away and said: "Good day, Mr. Oliver."

Oliver wandered from the Medical Center
into the business heart of the art colony. The
Van Gogh Works on the left must have
snagged the big order from Mexico—their

chimneys were going full blast and the reek of linseed oil and turps was strong in the air. But the poor buggers on the line at Rembrandts Ltd. across the square were out of luck. They'd been laid off for a month now, with no sign of a work call yet. Somebody jostled him off the sidewalk, somebody in a great hurry. Oliver sighed. The place was getting more like Chicago every day. He sometimes thought he had made art his line not because he had any special talent but because artists were relatively easygoing people, not so quick to pop you in the nose, not such aggressive drunks when they *were* drunks.

Quit the stalling, a thin, cold voice inside him said. Get over to Latham. The man said, "the sooner the better."

He went over to Latham whose waiting room was crowded with irascible women. After an hour he got to see the old man and hand him the slip.

Latham said: "Don't worry about a thing. Riordan's a good man. If he says it's operable, it's operable. Now we want Finsen to do the whittling. With Finsen operating, you won't have to worry about a thing. He's a good man. His fee's fifteen hundred."

"Oh, my God!" Oliver gulped.

"What's the matter—haven't you got it?"

To his surprise and terror, Oliver found himself giving Dr. Latham a hysterical stump speech about how he didn't have it and who did have it and how could anybody get ahead with the way prices were shooting up and everybody gouged you every time you turned around and, yes, that went for doctors too and if you did get a couple of als in your pocket the salesmen heard about it and battered at you until you put down an installment on some piece of junk you didn't want to get them out of your hair and what the hell kind of world was this anyway.

Latham listened, smiling and nodding, with, as Oliver finally realized, his hearing aid turned off. His voice ran down and Latham said briskly: "All right, then. You just come around when you've arranged the financial details and I'll contact Finsen. He's a good man; you won't have to worry about a thing. And remember: the sooner the better."

Oliver slumped out of the office and went straight to the Mob Building, office of the Regan Benevolent Fund. An acid-voiced woman there turned him down indignantly: "You should be ashamed of yourself trying to draw on the Fund when there are people in actual want who can't be accommodated! No, I don't want to hear any more about it if you please. There are others waiting."

Waiting for what? The same treatment?

Oliver realized with a shock that he hadn't phoned his foreman as promised, and it was four minutes to five. He did a dance of agonized impatience outside a telephone booth occupied by a fat woman. She noticed him, pursed her lips, hung up—and stayed in the booth. She began a slow search of her handbag, found coins and slowly dialed a new number. She gave him a malevolent grin as he walked away, crushed. He had a good job record, but that was no way to keep it good. One black mark, another black mark, and one day—bingo.

General Advances was open, of course. Through its window you could see handsome young men and sleek young women just waiting to help you, whatever the fiscal jam. He went in and was whisked to a booth where a big-bosomed honey-voiced blonde oozed sympathy over him. He walked out with a check for fifteen hundred alphs after signing countless papers, with the creamy hand of the girl on his to help guide the pen. What was printed on the papers, God and General Advances alone knew. There were men on the line who told him with resignation that they had been paying off to GA for the better part of their lives. There were men who said bitterly that GA was owned by the Regan Benevolent Fund, which must be a lie.

The street was full of people—strangers who didn't look like your run-of-the-mill artist. Muscle men, with the Chicago style and if anybody got one in the gut, too God-damned bad about it. They were peering into faces as they passed.

He was frightened. He stepped onto the slidewalk and hurried home, hoping for temporary peace there. But there was no peace for his frayed nerves. The apartment house door opened obediently when he told it: "Regan," but the elevator stood stupidly still when he said: "Seventh Floor." He spat bitterly and precisely: *"Sev-enth Floor."* The doors closed on him with a faintly derisive, pneumatic moan and he was whisked up to the eighth floor. He walked down wearily and said: "Cobalt blue" to his own door after a furtive look up and down the hall. It worked and he went to his phone to flash Latham, but didn't. Oliver sank instead into a dun-colored pneumatic chair, his 250-alph Hawthorne Electric Stepsaver door mike following him with its mindless snout. He punched a button on the chair and the 600-alph hi-fi selected a random tape. A long, pure melodic trumpet line filled the room. It died for two beats and then the strings and woodwinds picked it up and tossed it—

Oliver snapped off the music, sweat starting from his brow. It was the Gershwin "Lost Symphony," and he remembered how Gershwin had died. There had been a little nodule in his brain as there was a little nodule in Oliver's throat.

Time, the Great Kidder. The years drifted by. Suddenly you were middle-aged, running to the medics for this and that. Suddenly they told you to have your throat whittled out or die disgustingly. And what did you have to show for it? A number, a travel pass, a payment book from General Advances, a bunch of junk you never wanted, a job that was a heavier ball and chain than any convict ever wore in the barbarous days of Government. Was this what Regan and Falcaro had bled for?

He defrosted some hamburger, fried it and ate it and then went mechanically down to the tavern. He didn't like to drink every night, but you had to be one of the boys, or word would get back to the plant and you might be on your way to another black mark. They were racing under the lights at Hawthorne too, and he'd be expected to put a couple of ales down. He never seemed to win. Nobody he knew ever seemed to win. Not at the horses, not at the craps table, not at the numbers.

He stood outside the neon-bright saloon for a long moment, and then turned and walked into the darkness away from town, possessed by impulses he did not understand or want to understand. He had only a vague hope that standing on the Dunes and looking out across the dark lake might somehow soothe him.

In half an hour he had reached the deciduous forest, then the pine, then the scrubby brushes, then the grasses, then the bare white sand. And lying in it he found two people: a man so hard and dark he seemed to be carved from oak and a woman so white and gaunt she seemed to be carved from ivory.

He turned shyly from the woman.

"Are you all right?" he asked the man. "Is there anything I can do?"

The man opened red-rimmed eyes. "Better leave us alone," he said. "We'd only get you into trouble."

Oliver laughed hysterically. "Trouble?" he said. "Don't think of it."

The man seemed to be measuring him with his eyes, and said at last: "You'd better go and not talk about us. We're enemies of the Mob."

Oliver said after a pause: "So am I. Don't go away. I'll be back with some clothes and food for you and the lady. Then I can help you to my place. I'm an enemy of the Mob too. I just never knew it until now."

He started off and then turned. "You won't go away? I mean it. I want to help you. I can't seem to help myself, but perhaps there's something—"

The man said tiredly: "We won't go away."

Oliver hurried off. There was something mingled with the scent of the pine forest to-night. He was halfway home before he identi-fied it: oil smoke.

TWENTY

Lee swore and said: "I can get up if I want to."

"You'll stay in bed whether you want to or not," Charles told her. "You're a sick woman."

"I'm a very bad-tempered woman and that means I'm convalescent. Ask anybody."

"I'll go right out into the street and do that, darling."

She got out of bed and wrapped Oliver's dressing gown around her. "I'm hungry again," she said.

"He'll be back soon. You've left nothing but some frozen—worms, looks like. Shall I defrost them?"

"Please don't trouble. I can wait."

"Window!" he snapped.

She ducked back and swore again, this time at herself. "Sorry," she said. "Which will do us a whole hell of a lot of good if somebody saw me and started wondering."

Oliver came in with packages. Lee kissed him and he grinned shyly. "Trout," he whispered. She grabbed the packages and flew to the kitchenette.

"The way to Lee Falcaro's heart," Charles mused. "How's your throat, Ken?"

"No pain, today," Oliver whispered. "Latham says I can talk as much as I like. And I've got things to talk about." He opened his coat and hauled out a flat package that had been stuffed under his belt. "Stolen from the factory. Brushes, pens, tubes of ink, drawing instruments. My friends, you are going to return to Syndic Territory in style, with passes and permits galore."

Lee returned. "Trout's frying," she said. "I heard that about the passes. Are you *sure* you can fake them?"

His face fell. "Eight years at the Chicago Art Institute," he whispered. "Three years at Original Reproductions, Inc. Eleven years at Picasso Oils and Etchings, where I am now third figure man in the Blue Department. I really think I deserve your confidence."

"Ken, we trust and love you. If it weren't for the difference in your ages I'd marry you *and* Charles. Now what about the Chicagoans? Hold it—the fish?"

Dinner was served and cleared away before they could get more out of Oliver. His throat wasn't ready for more than one job at a time. He told them at last: "Things are quieting down. There are still some strangers in town and the road patrols are still acting very hard-boiled. But nobody's been pulled in today.

Somebody told me on the line that the whole business is a lot of foolishness. He said the ship must have been damaged by somebody's stupidity and Regan must have been killed in a brawl—everybody knows he was half-crazy, like his father. So my friend figures they made up the story about two wild Europeans to cover up a mess. I said I thought there was a lot in what he said." Oliver laughed silently.

"Good man!" Charles tried not to act over-eager. "When do you think you can start on the passes, Ken?"

Oliver's face dropped a little. "Tonight," he whispered. "I don't suppose the first couple of tries will be any good so—let's go."

Lee put her hand on his shoulder. "We'll miss you too," she said. "But don't ever forget this: we're coming back. Hell won't stop us. We're coming back."

Oliver was arranging stolen instruments on the table. "You have a big order," he whispered sadly. "I guess you aren't afraid of it because you've always been rich and strong. Anything you want to do you think you can do. But those government people? And after them the Mob? Maybe it would be better if you just let things take their course, Lee. I've found out a person can be happy even here."

"We're coming back," Lee said.

Oliver took out his own Michigan City-Chicago travel permit. As always, the sight of it made Charles wince. Americans under such a yoke! Oliver whispered: "I got a good long look today at a Michigan City-Buffalo permit. The foreman's. He buys turps from Carolina at Buffalo. I sketched it from memory as soon as I got by myself. I don't swear to it, not yet, but I have the sketch to practice from and I can get a few more looks later."

He pinned down the drawing paper, licked a ruling pen and filled it, and began to copy the border of his own pass.

"I don't suppose there's anything I can do?" Lee asked.

"You can turn on the audio," Oliver whispered. "They have it going all the time at the shop. I don't feel right working unless there's some music driving me out of my mind."

Lee turned on the big Hawthorne Electric set with a wave of her hand; imbecilic music filled the air and Oliver grunted and settled down.

Lee and Charles listened, fingers entwined, to half an hour of slushy ballads while Oliver worked. The news period announcer came on with some anesthetic trial verdicts, sports results and society notes about which Regan had gone where. Then—

"The local Mobsters of Michigan City, Indiana, today welcomed Maurice Regan to their town. Mr. Regan will assume direction of efforts to apprehend the two European savages who murdered James Regan IV last month aboard the ore boat *Hon. James J. Regan* in waters off Michigan City. You probably remember that the Europeans did some damage to the vessel's reactor room before they fled from the ship. How they boarded the ship and their present whereabouts are mysteries—but they probably won't be mysteries long. Maurice Regan is little known to the public, but he has built an enviable record in the administration of the Chicago Police Department. Mr. Regan on taking charge of the case, said this: 'We know by traces found on the Dunes that they got away. We know from the logs of highway patrols that they didn't get out of the Michigan City area. The only way to close the books on this matter fast is to cover the city with a fine-tooth comb. Naturally and unfortunately this will mean inconvenience to many citizens. I hope they will bear with the inconveniences gladly for the sake of confining those two savages in a place where they can no longer be a menace. I have methods of my own and there may be complaints. Reasonable suggestions will be heeded, but with crackpots I have no patience.''

The radio began to spew more sports results. Oliver turned and waved at it to be silent. "I don't like that," he whispered. "I never heard of this Regan in the Chicago Police."

"They said he wasn't in the public eye."

"I wasn't the public. I did some posters for the Police and I knew who was who. And that bit at the end. I've heard things like it before. The Mob doesn't often admit it's in the wrong, you know. When they try to disarm criticism in advance . . . this Regan must be a rough fellow."

Charles and Lee Falcaro looked at each other in sudden fear. "We don't want to hurry you, Ken," she said. "But it looks as though you'd better do a rush job."

Nodding, Oliver bent over the table. "Maybe a week," he said hopefully. With the finest pen he traced the curlicues an engraving lathe had evolved to make the passes foolproof. Odd, he thought—the lives of these two hanging by such a weak thing as the twisted thread of color that feeds from pen to paper. And, as an afterthought—I suppose mine does too.

Oliver came back the next day to work with concentrated fury, barely stopping to eat and not stopping to talk. Lee got it out of him, but not easily. After being trapped in a half-dozen contradictions about feeling well and having a headache, about his throat being sore and the pain having gone, he put down his pen and whispered steadily: "I didn't want you to worry, friends. But it looks bad. There is a new crowd in town. Twenty couples have been pulled in by them—*couples*—to prove who they were. Maybe fifty people have been pulled in for questioning—what do you know about this, what do you know about that. And they've begun house searches. Anybody you don't like, you tell the new Regan about him. Say he's sheltering Europeans. And his people pull them in. Why, everybody wants to know, are they pulling in couples who are obviously American if they're looking for Europeans? And, everybody says, they've never seen anything like it. Now—I think I'd better get back to work."

"Yes," Lee said. "I think you had."

Charles was at the window, peering around

the drawn blind. "Look at that," he said to Lee. She came over. A big man on the street below was walking, very methodically, down the street.

"I will bet you," Charles said, "that he'll be back this way in ten minutes or so—and so on through the night."

"I won't take the bet," she said. "He's a sentry, all right. The Mob's learning from their friends across the water. Learning too damned much. They must be all over town."

They watched at the window and the sentry was back in ten minutes. On his fifth tour he stopped a young couple going down the street, studied their faces, drew a gun on them and blew a whistle. A patrol came and took them away; the girl was hysterical. At two in the morning, the sentry was relieved by another, just as big and just as dangerous looking. At two in the morning they were still watching and Oliver was still hunched over the table tracing exquisite filigrees of color.

In five days, virtually without sleep, Oliver finished two Michigan City-Buffalo travel permits. The apartment house next door was hit by raiders while the ink dried; Charles and Lee Falcaro stood waiting, grotesquely armed with kitchen knives. But it must have been a tip rather than part of the search plan crawling nearer to their end of town. The raiders did not hit their building.

Oliver had bought clothes according to Lee's instructions—including two men's suits, Oliver's size. One she let out for

Charles; the other she took in for herself. She
instructed Charles minutely in how he was to
behave on the outside. First he roared with
incredulous laughter; Lee, wise in psychology, assured him that she was perfectly
serious. Oliver, puzzled by his näiveté,
assured him that such things were not un-
common—not at least in Mob Territory.
Charles then roared with indignation and Lee
roared him down. His last broken protest
was: "But what'll I do if somebody takes me
up on it?"

She shrugged, washing her hands of the
matter, and went on trimming and dyeing her
hair.

It was morning when she kissed Oliver
good-by, said to Charles: "See you at the station. Don't say good-by," and walked from the
apartment, a dark-haired boy with a slight
limp. Charles watched her down the street. A
cop turned to look after her and then went on
his way.

Half an hour later Charles shook hands
with Oliver and went out.

Oliver didn't go to work that day. He sat all
day at the table, drawing endless slow
sketches of Lee Falcaro's head.

Time, the Great Kidder, he thought. He
opens the door that shows you in the next
room tables of goodies, colorful and tasty,
men and women around the tables pleasantly
surprised to see you, beckoning to you to join
the feast. We have roast beef if you're serious,
we have caviar if you're experimental, we
have baked alaska if you're frivolous—join

the feast; try a little bit of everything. So you start toward the door.

Time, the Great Kidder, pulls the rug from under your feet and slams the door while the guests at the feast laugh their heads off at your painful but superficial injuries.

Oliver slowly drew Lee's head for the fifteenth time and wished he dared to turn on the audio for the news. Perhaps, he thought, the next voice you hear will be the gunmen at the door.

TWENTY-ONE

Charles walked down the street and ran immediately into a challenge from a police sergeant.

"Where you from, mister?" the cop demanded, balanced and ready to draw.

Charles gulped and let Lee Falcaro's drilling take over. "Oh, around, sergeant. I'm from around here."

"What're you so nervous about?"

"Why, sergeant, you're such an exciting type, really. Did anybody ever tell you you look well in uniform?"

The cop glared at him and said: "If I wasn't in uniform, I'd hang one on you, sister. And if the force wasn't all out hunting the lunatics that killed Mr. Regan I'd pull you in for spitting on the sidewalk. Get to hell off my beat and stay off. I'm not forgetting your face."

Charles scurried on. It had worked.

It worked once more with a uniformed

policeman. One of the Chicago plain-clothes imports was the third and last. He socked Charles in the jaw and sent him on his way with a kick in the rear. He had been thoroughly warned that it would probably happen: "Count on them to over-react. That's the key to it. You'll make them so eager to assert their own virility, that it'll temporarily bury their primary mission. It's quite likely that one or more pokes will be taken at you. All you can do is take them. If you get—*when* you get through they'll be cheap at the price."

The sock in the jaw hadn't been very expert. The kick in the pants was negligible, considering the fact that it had propelled him through the gate of the Michigan City Transport Terminal.

By the big terminal clock the Chicago-Buffalo Express was due in fifteen minutes. Its gleaming single rail, as tall as a man, crossed the far end of the concourse. Most of the fifty-odd people in the station were probably Buffalo-bound . . . safe geldings who could be trusted to visit Syndic Territory, off the leash, and return obediently. Well-dressed, of course, and many past middle age, with a stake in the Mob Territory stronger than hope of freedom. One youngster, though —oh. It was Lee, leaning, slack-jawed, against a pillar and reading the Green Sheet.

Who were the cops in the crowd? The thick-set man with restless eyes, of course. The saintly looking guy who kept moving and glancing into faces.

Charles went to the newsstand and put a

coin in the slot for *The Mob—A Short History*, by the same B. Arrowsmith Hynde who had brightened and misinformed his youth.

Nothing to it, he thought. Train comes in, put your money in the turnstile, show your permit to the turnstile's eye, get aboard and that—is—that. Unless the money is phony, or the pass is phony in which case the turnstile locks and all hell breaks loose. His money was just dandy, but the permit now—there hadn't been any way to test it against a turnstile's template, or time to do it if there had been a way. Was the probability of boarding two to one?

The probability abruptly dropped to zero as a round little man flanked by two huge men entered the station.

Commander Grinnel.

The picture puzzle fell into a whole as the two plain-clothes men circulating in the station eyed Grinnel and nodded to him. The big one absent-mindedly made a gesture that was the start of a police salute.

Grinnel was Maurice Regan—the Maurice Regan mysteriously unknown to Oliver, who knew the Chicago Police. Grinnel was a bit of a lend-lease from the North American Navy, called in because of his unique knowledge of Charles Orsino and Lee Falcaro, their faces, voices and behavior. Grinnel was the expert in combing the city without any nonsense about rights and mouthpieces. Grinnel was the expert who could set up a military interior guard of the city. Grinnel was the specialist temporarily invested with the rank of a Regan so he could do his job.

The round little man with the halo of hair walked briskly to the turnstile and there stood at a military parade rest with a look of resignation on his face.

How hard on me it is, he seemed to be saying, that I have such dull damn duty. How hard that an officer of my brilliance must do sentry-go for every train to Syndic Territory.

The slack-jawed youth who was Lee Falcaro looked at him over her Green Sheet and nodded before dipping into the Tia Juana past performances again. She knew.

Passengers were beginning to line up at the turnstile, smoothing out their money and fiddling with their permits. In a minute he and Lee Falcaro would have to join the line or stand conspicuously on the emptying floor. The thing was dead for twenty-four hours now, until the next train—and then Grinnel headed across the floor looking very impersonal. The look of a man going to the men's room. The station cops and Grinnel's two bruisers drifted together at the turnstile and began to chat.

Charles followed Grinnel, wearing the same impersonal look and entered the room almost on his heels.

Grinnel saw him in a washbowl mirror; simultaneously he half-turned, opened his mouth to yell and whipped his hand into his coat. A single roundhouse right from Charles crunched into the soft side of his neck. He fell with his head twisted at an odd angle. Blood began to run from the corner of his mouth onto his shirt.

"Remember Martha?" Charles whispered down at the body. "That was for Martha." He looked around the tiled room. There was a mop closet with the door ajar, and Grinnel's flabby body fitted in it.

Charles walked from the washroom to the line of passengers across the floor. It seemed to go on for miles. Lee Falcaro was no longer lounging against the post. He spotted her in line, still slack-jawed, still gaping over the magazine. The monorail began to sing shrilly with the vibration of the train braking a mile away, and the turnstile "unlocked" light went on.

There was the usual number of fumblers, the usual number of "please unfold your currency" flashes. Lee carried through to the end with her slovenly pose. For her the sign said: "incorrect denominations." Behind her a man snarled: "For Christ's sake, kid, we're all waiting on you!" The cops only half noticed; they were talking. When Charles got to the turnstile one of the cops was saying: "Maybe it's something he ate. How *you* like somebody to barge in—"

The rest was lost in the clicking of the turnstile that led him through.

He settled in a very pneumatic chair as the train accelerated evenly to a speed of three hundred and fifty miles per hour. A sign in the car said that the next stop was Buffalo. And there was Lee, lurching up the aisle against the acceleration. She spotted him, tossed the Green Sheet in the Air and fell into his lap.

"Disgusting!" snarled a man across the aisle. "Simply disgusting!"

"You haven't seen anything yet," Lee told him, and kissed Charles on the mouth.

The man choked: "I shall certainly report this to the authorities when we arrive in Buffalo!"

"Mmm," said Lee, preoccupied. "Do that, mister. Do that."

TWENTY-TWO

"I didn't like his reaction," Charles told her in the anteroom of F. W. Taylor's office. "I didn't talk to him long on the phone, but I didn't like his reaction at all. He seemed to think I was exaggerating. Or all wet. Or a punk kid."

"I can assure him you're not that," Lee Falcaro said warmly. "Call on me any time."

He gave her a worried smile. The door opened then and they went in.

Uncle Frank looked up. "We'd just about written you two off," he said. "What's it like?"

"Bad," Charles said. "Worse than anything you've imagined. There's an underground, all right, and they are practicing assassination."

"Too bad," the old man said. "We'll have to shake up the bodyguard organization. Make 'em de rigeur at all hours, screen 'em and see that they really know how to shoot. I hate to meddle, but we can't have the Government knocking our people off."

"It's worse than that," Lee said. "There's a tie-up between the Government and the Mob. We got away from Ireland aboard a speed boat and we were picked up by a Mob lakes ore ship. It had been running gasoline and ammunition to the Government. Jimmy Regan was in charge of the deal. We jumped into Lake Michigan and made our way back here. We were in Mob Territory—down among the smalltimers—long enough to establish that the Mob and Government are hand in glove. One of these days they're going to jump us."

"Ah," Taylor said softly. "I've thought so for a long time."

Charles burst out: "Then for God's sake, Uncle Frank, why haven't you *done* anything? You don't know what it's like out there. The Government's a nightmare. They have slaves. And the Mob's not much better. Numbers! Restrictions! Permits! Passes! And they don't call it that, but they have . . . government!"

"They're mad," Lee said. "Quite mad. And I'm talking technically. Neurotics and psychotics swarm in the streets of Mob Territory. The Government, naturally—but the Mob was a shock. We've got to get ready, Mr. Taylor. Every psychotic or severe neurotic in Syndic Territory is a potential agent of theirs."

"Don't just check off the Government, darling," Charles said tensely. "They've got to be smashed. They're no good to themselves or anybody else. Life's a burden there if only they knew it. And they're holding down the natives by horrible cruelty."

Taylor leaned back and asked: "What do you recommend?"

Charles said: "A fighting fleet and an army."

Lee said: "Mass diagnosis of the unstable. Screening of severe cases and treatment when it's indicated. Riveredge must be a plague-spot of agents."

Taylor shook his head and told them: "It won't do."

Charles was aghast. "It won't *do*? Uncle Frank, what the hell do you mean, it won't do? Didn't we make it clear? They want to invade us and loot us and subject us!"

"It won't do," Taylor said. "I choose the devil we know. A fighting fleet is out. We'll arm our merchant vessels and hope for the best. A full-time army is out. We'll get together some kind of militia. And a roundup of the unstable is out."

"Why?" Lee demanded. "My people have worked out perfectly effective techniques—"

"Let me talk, please. I have a feeling that it won't be any good, but hear me out.

"I'll take your black art first, Lee. As you know, I have played with history. To a historian, your work has been very interesting. The sequence was this: study of abnormal psychology collapsed under Lieberman's findings, study of abnormal psychology revived by you when you invalidated Lieberman's findings. I suggest that Lieberman and his followers were correct—and that you were correct. I suggest that what changed was the make-up of the population. That would mean that before Lieberman there were plenty of neurotics and psychotics to study, that in Lieberman's time there were so few that earlier generalizations were invalidated, and that now—in our time, Lee—neurotics and psychotics are among us again in increasingly ample numbers."

The girl opened her mouth, shut it again and thoughtfully studied her nails.

"I will not tolerate," Taylor went on, "a roundup or a registration, or mass treatment or any such violation of the Syndic's spirit."

Charles exploded: "Damn it, this is a matter of life or death to the Syndic!"

"No, Charles. Nothing can be a matter of life or death to the Syndic. When anything becomes a matter of life or death to the Syndic, the Syndic is already dead, its morale is already disintegrated, its credit already gone. What is left is not the Syndic but the Syndic's dead shell. I am not placed so that I can say objectively now whether the Syndic is dead or alive. I fear it is dying. The rising tide of neurotics is a symptom. The suggestion from you two, who should be imbued with the old happy-go-lucky, we-can't-miss esprit of the Syndic, that we cower behind mercenaries instead of trusting the people who made us— that's another symptom. Dick Reiner's rise to influence on a policy of driving the Government from the seas is another symptom.

"I mentioned the devil we know as my choice. That's the status quo, even though I have reason to fear it's crumbling beneath our feet. If it is, it may last out our time. We'll shore it up with armed merchantmen and a militia. If the people are with us now as they always have been, that'll do it. The devil we don't know is what we'll become if we radically dislocate Syndic life and attitudes.

"I can't back a fighting fleet. I can't back a regular army. I can't back any restrictive measure on the freedom of anybody but an apprehended criminal. Read history. It has taught me not to meddle, it has taught me that no man should think himself clever enough or good enough to dare it.

"Who can know what he's doing when he doesn't even know why he does it? Bless the bright Cro-Magnon for inventing the bow and damn him for inventing missile warfare. Bless the stubby little Sumerians for miracles of beauty in gold and lapis lazuli and damn them for burying a dead queen's hand-maidens alive in her tomb. Bless Shih Huang Ti for building the Great Wall between northern barbarism and southern culture, and damn him for burning every book in China. Bless King Minos for the ease of Knossian flush toilets and damn him for his yearly tribute of Greek sacrificial victims. Bless Pharaoh for peace and damn him for slavery. Bless the Greeks for restricting population so the well-fed few could kindle a watch-tower in the West, and damn the prostitution and sodomy and wars of colonization and infanticide by which they did it. Bless the Romans for their strength to smash down every wall that hemmed their genius, and damn them for their weakness that never broke the bloody grip of Etruscan savagery on their minds. Bless the Jews who discovered the fatherhood of God and damn them who limited it to the survivors of a surgical operation. Bless the Christians who abolished the surgical preliminaries and damn them who substituted a thousand cerebral quibbles. Bless Justinian for the Code of Law and damn him for his countless treacheries that were the prototype of the wretched Byzantine millenium. Bless the churchmen for teaching and preaching, and damn them for drawing a line beyond which they could only teach and preach in peril of the stake.

"Bless the navigators who opened the new world to famine-ridden Europe, and damn them for syphilis. Bless the Redskins who bred maize the great preserver of life, and damn them for breeding maize the great destroyer of top-soil. Bless the Virginia planters for the solace of tobacco and damn them for the cancer and red gullies they left where forests had stood. Bless the obstetricians with forceps who eased the agony of labor and damn them for bringing countless monsters into the world to reproduce their kind. Bless the do-gooders who slew the malaria mosquitoes of Ceylon and damn them for letting more Singhalese be born than five Ceylons could feed. Bless the founding fathers for the exquisitely Newtonian eighteenth-century machinery of the Constitution, and curse them for visiting it in all its unworkable beauty on the nineteenth, twentieth and twenty-first centuries.

"Who knows what he is doing, why he does it or what the consequences will be?

"Let the social scientists play with their theories if they like; I'm fond of poetry myself. The fact is that they have not so far solved what I call the billion-body problem. With brilliant hindsight some of them tell us that more than a dozen civilizations have gone into the darkness before us. I see no reason why ours should not go down into the darkness with them, nor do I see any reason why we should not meanwhile enjoy ourselves collecting sense impressions to be remembered with pleasure in old age. No; I will not agitate for extermination of the Government and hegemony over the Mob. Such a policy would automatically, inevitably and immediately entail many, many violent deaths and painful wounds. The wrong kind of sense impressions. I shall, with fear and trembling, recommend the raising of a militia—a purely defensive, extremely sloppy militia—and pray that it will not involve us in a war of aggression."

He looked at the two of them and shrugged. "Lee so stern, Charles so grim," he said. "I suppose you're dedicated now. I have a faint desire to take the pistol from my desk and shoot you both. I have a nervous feeling that you're about to embark on a crusade to awaken Syndic Territory to its perils. You think the fate of civilization hinges on you. You're right, of course. The fate of civilization hinges on every one of us at any given moment. We are all components in the four-billion-body problem. Somehow for a century we've achieved in Syndic Territory for almost everybody the civil liberties, peace of mind and living standards that were enjoyed by the middle class before 1914—plus longer life, better health, a more generous morality, increased command over nature, and minus the servant problem and certain superstitions. A handful of wonderfully pleasant decades. When you look back over history you wonder who in his right mind could ask for more. And you wonder who would dare to presume to tamper with it." He paused and studied the earnest young faces. There was so much more that he might say—but he shrugged again.

"Bless you," he said. "Gather ye sense impressions while ye may. Some like pointer readings, some like friction on the mucous membranes. Different people get their kicks different ways. Now go about your dark and bloody business; I have work to do."

He didn't really. When he was alone he leaned back and laughed and laughed.

Win, lose or draw, those two would go far and enjoy themselves mightily along the way.

Afterword — THE SYNDIC

When Cyril Kornbluth died, he left a number of incomplete writing projects. Most writers have drawers full of the things. It is part of the inevitable fallout of the writing profession. You start a story and run out of inspiration; so you put it away. You are in the middle of a story and something comes up with an urgent deadline, so you put that one aside, too. You get well into a story and, after a lot of it is on paper, it no longer looks as good as it had seemed in contemplation—in all these ways, fragments accumulate.

Cyril, who was a more methodical human being than most of us, had relatively few of these literary fragments. Still, there were enough so that, over a period of some years, I was able to finish about a dozen of them up and get them into print. One of them, *The Meeting*, won a Hugo at the World Science Fiction Convention in Toronto in 1973—fifteen years after Cyril's death. About time, I thought; although actually the principal reason that Cyril Kornbluth did not collect a shelf full of Hugos and Nebulas was only that for most of his writing career the awards did not yet exist.

The best measure of a writer's repute in those days was probably the esteem in which he was held by editors. By that measure Cyril had few peers.

There are writers who are good. There are writers who are fast. There are writers who are dependable. They are very seldom the same writer. Most fallible human beings can manage to get something done on time, or to do it well; Cyril managed to combine all these traits, superlatively. Among the editors Cyril worked with were Horace Gold, Robert P. Mills, John Campbell, Donald A. Wollheim, Robert A. W. Lowndes and myself, and all of them remember him with respect. (In fact, Horace Gold has written a memoir for this volume, which will follow these notes.) In the days when Cyril Kornbluth was the darling of the editors the editors themselves were a more significant force in the field of science fiction than in most kinds of writing—more than they are now, perhaps, when there are so many more of them that few individuals stand out. So it was not surprising that Cyril Kornbluth decided to see what the view looked like from the other side of the desk.

Most writers daydream about changing roles. They look across the desk at the person who can say yes or no to a check or a contract, and speculate about what it would be like to move over to the side where the power is. Most writers, however, then stop to think about the price that has to be paid for that power. The price is not low. It entails things like having to go to an office and worrying about printers and artists and circulation people; it may even entail having to shave every day. And there is also the question of money. Editors are not usually welfare clients, but no editor ever comes close to the kind of income a first-rate writer can command.

Nevertheless, Cyril finally came to feel that it was fair for him to take his turn in the barrel. He accepted a post on the editorial staff of *The Magazine of Fantasy and Science Fiction*.

His first duties were to wade through the "slush pile"—that accumulation of unasked-for stories that is both the bane and the hope of an editor's life. Almost all of it is garbage, but it is also the place where you find the Heinleins and the LeGuins and the Asimovs of the next generation. Cyril took to the work with pleasure. I remember him ecstatically quoting to me lines from Fritz Leiber's story, *The Silver Eggheads*, which he had been the editor to buy after graduating from the slush pile. I suspect that if he had lived long enough, and had stayed with editing, he would have been one of the great ones. He had enthusiasm, intelligence, diligence and taste—that just about defines the talents that join to make the best editors.

But he didn't survive to make his mark.

I ran into Cyril by accident at Horace Gold's home, not long before his death. It was unplanned. I was delivering a manuscript and Cyril on some vague errand which he did not seem to want to define. (I didn't find out just what he had been doing until I read the memoir that follows.) Cyril and I left together, walked up to Pennsylvania Station, had a couple of beers while we were waiting for our trains and then went our separate ways, Cyril to Long Island and me to New Jersey.

A very short time later (it seems in retrospect, anyway) Mary Kornbluth called, weeping, to say that Cyril had got up that morning, rushed to catch a train with a bundle of manuscripts for *F&SF* and died on the platform of the Long Island Railroad station.

— Frederik Pohl

A PERSONAL NOTE
by H.L. Gold

It's difficult to think back to my first en-
counter with C.M. Kornbluth. It's impossible
to forget our last. The years between were
filled high with public triumph and private
tragedy for both of us. I wish I could remember one and not the other, but his tragedy
finally killed him and mine just barely missed
—yet ironically he, the dead, grows ever more
famous, while I, the living, am known to pro-
gressively fewer and fewer people. So sober-
ing is this fact that it has made me perhaps
the best-qualified person to introduce you to
the author.

But first I find I must answer this question
for the younger readers: Who am I?

Well, practically nobody now and not much
better known in 1950, when I started *Galaxy*
magazine. For an idea of how unlikely that
was, the publisher was European and didn't
know what a galaxy was, and the editor had

some know-how but little know-who, not having written, edited or even read science fiction in over a decade. A pretty funny combination, eh?

But only a publisher with no knowlege of the field would give the backing I asked for— to pay double the going word rate, to buy only first-magazine rights instead of all rights, as the competition demanded, to eschew naked maidens and bad-tasting ads from cover to cover — to put out, in short, a handsome, mature magazine that readers wouldn't feel ashamed to carry and that writers and artists might be glad to contribute to.

The funny combination worked. *Galaxy* was in the black with its fifth issue, a record in any field. So, far from feeling ashamed, readers declared themselves proud to be seen carrying it, and writers and artists who had abandoned science fiction in boredom or disgust came crowding back, while I, not knowing one name from another, read everything that flooded in — letters, postcards, telegrams, manuscripts—and I kept doing that all my eleven years as editor.

Perhaps my best source of stories was Frederik Pohl's literary agency. He had sold me "The Marching Morons" by one C.M. Kornbluth and now I asked for some information about the author. Fred obliged and I learned that the *C* stood for Cyril, that he was married, was in his late 20s and worked for a wire service in Chicago, where he filed 15,000 words of news a day—then went home and wrote stories nights and weekends.

I was horrified. Why, if Kornbluth would write 5,000 words of fiction a *week*, I told Pohl, he could earn a lot more than he was making. Fred said that was what he was trying to convince him of. Then came our almost daily routine: When would he, Frederik Pohl, write the book-length serial he had outlined to me in a rash moment, under his own name, not the pseudonym he had used years back? I expected him to say he'd think about it. He had always said that. But this time was different. Cyril Kornbluth, he said, was moving to New York and they were going to collaborate on the story.

It takes will power not to stud that paragraph with exclamation points, but all I said at the moment was great, wonderful, you'll never regret it—not knowing how great and wonderful it would be—and when can we get started? Very soon, said Fred, and very soon indeed they came to the apartment in which I did my editing.

When Cyril and I shook hands and sat down, I looked over this prodigy who could manufacture 75,000 words of news a week—enough for a good-sized book—and still write stories at home. I don't recall what I saw that day, for my view of him never stopped changing.

His widow, Mary, is my authority for the statements that he was shorter and broader than I remember, that his eyes seldom widened behind their heavy lenses except when he laughed, generally at someone's expense, but I forgot to ask her the color of his hair and whether he had much or little. I don't need to be reminded of his stinging wit, but Mary again is my authority—the more discomfited he was, the deeper it bit—and that I made him unusually uncomfortable, for he stung me more than most ... until his last visit with me, which I'll come to in a while.

I wonder if they suspected, any more than I did, how much bigger the moment was than just the hard decision each had made? For out of that meeting came the byline, Frederik Pohl & C.M. Kornbluth, that was to change the whole course of science fiction with their first serial, now known (and available) in book form as "The Space Merchants."

While they wrote together, I had first look at everything they produced, buying most of it and rejecting very little, if any, and we met often for story conferences. Then Fred struck out on his own and Cyril collaborated with Judith Merril on a couple of serials, selling one to *Galaxy* and the other to *Astounding*, before going his own way. I continued to get first refusal from Fred, but not from Cyril. What was wrong? Why wouldn't he let me see his work?

It wasn't for lack of my trying. I called his Long Island home at least once a month, invariably getting Mary instead of him, and she gave me the sad news of his failing heart, raddled by the war. He couldn't, she said, take traveling to New York as often as story conferences would require. Another was my own overeagerness to get the best for *Galaxy*; as Fred Pohl said, I often got the story but lost the author.

Until "The Space Merchants" appeared,

Utopias had been left to Socialists and intellectuals, who foresaw peace and sweet reason if only the world would listen. But Pohl and Kornbluth took the opposite tack. Imagine, they said, a world of free enterprise carried to its Nth degree, when even the armed forces and postal system belonged to the most powerful and competitive corporations. With that as their premise, they fashioned a future so credible in its sociology, legal structure, culture and customs that the reader felt he could live in it, however unpleasant it might be.

And that was the revolutionary point of the story: Any Utopia rewards some of its citizens and punishes others, in this case a heaven for capitalists and hell for Socialists, whereas it had always been the other way round.

From "The Space Merchants" on, science fiction found, at least in *Galaxy*, a nearly bottomless source of such reversed premises, on Earth as well as off among the stars, with their sociologies and psychologies rendered in depth and all conflict based squarely on their own extrapolations, instead of being limited to ours.

While Kornbluth and Pohl wrote together, which was a number of years, it was impossible to tell who produced what parts of any story, so closely did they work. I bought most, if not all, of their prolific output, and we met often, socially as well as professionally. Yet I can't say I got to know Cyril. Maybe nobody did, including his wife and collaborator, for the way he comes to mind is as an outwardly friendly porcupine who pricked you if you tried to get too close. Well, nobody had to love an editor, any more than an editor had to love all his contributors, so long as there was commerce between them. The important thing was their stories, which helped *Galaxy* break all sorts of new ground.

Then came the so-called boom in science fiction, caused largely by *Galaxy*'s astonishing success, when publishers who should have known better and neo-publishers who didn't thought they could make a mint by offering our best rates, *sight unseen*, to our top authors. You might think that should have broken us. Instead, our circulation continued to rise. The newcomers died and our authors came back to us—but not Cyril Kornbluth.

When I called one day, however, he took the phone from Mary and told me he had just become editor of *Fantasy & Science Fiction* and could he come talk editing with me? I said sure, of course, congratulations and you name it, which he did.

He came early on the appointed day, looking like a sick man, but not as sick as he proved to be. We had a second breakfast and then I told him to shoot questions at me. He'd gone through the pile of manuscripts he had inherited, he said, and were my submissions so much better than his? The only way to answer was to let him scan my pile. He looked up in bewilderment. How could I put out *Galaxy* with such overwritten, underdeveloped stories?

I took him step by step through revised

stories, edited copy, galley sheets with additional changes, and more changes in the final proofs. He read them minutely, nodding when he approved, grunting when he didn't. It felt good to see the nods outnumber the grunts.

"So," he said at last, "What's the trick?"

"Publish better stories than the ones you receive," I said.

Didn't any manuscripts come in in usable shape? Certainly, a good chunk of each issue, among them many fresh and memorable stories—but the rest of each issue had to be sweated for, my sweat as well as the authors'.

We had lunch and then went through the writing of blurbs, teasers for the next issue, style sheets and house ads—everything but copy and proofreading marks, which he had learned in Chicago. I had him call Mary and tell her he was having dinner with me. He ate in silence, digesting more than his food. Finished, he asked me to quiz him. I did, sharply. He answered correctly almost every time, an astonishing feat of attention span and absorption.

Finally, he got up to leave, stopped, turned around and asked if I were too tired to discuss an idea for a whole series of related stories. No, go ahead, I said, and as he talked and I threw in suggestions, we took an exciting kind of creative fire from each other. It always happened to me and now it was happening to Cyril, and it made him say, when the first story had been plotted and I'd given him the promise of an advance on a few written chapters, that he had been an idiot to work for low rates when he could have sold to *Galaxy* for so much more. I assured him that I had done the same thing until becoming an editor, that I regretted not having had his stories but that I had no hard feelings and was looking forward to the series and anything else he cared to submit. He asked if I would write for *F & SF* and I assured him I would—*and would do any revisions he might want!* We grinned and shook hands and he went out into the wintery night.

We had spent ten long, crowded hours together, a day of warm but terrible gentleness between us. It should have exhausted him, a cardiac with so few physical reserves, and me, living on nervous energy as if it were bottomless—yet he went home to read manuscripts with his new-found insights while I spent the rest of the night catching up on deadlines. If only, I thought, all writers could make editing part of their basic training! It had taken Cyril and me so long to learn the fundamental first laws of publishing: that the editor's job is to buy, not reject, that every good magazine is a seller's market, and that editing is hard on the writer but harder still on the editor, who must encourage, coax, wheedle, use any means to induce the writer to do his best, without losing him—and not just one writer but as many as he can find.

Before I went to bed the next afternoon, Mary phoned. Cyril had just gone to sleep, but not until he had promised that their hardships were behind them. She had never seen him so buoyant and self-confident. What magic had I wrought? None, I told her, that hadn't been wrought innumerable times for me, as writer, as editor, and as reader. What, editors *read*? Wait and see, I said, and hung up and went blissfully to sleep.

I don't remember who told me, Mary or Fred Pohl, maybe neither, that Cyril was dead, so few days later. *How*, I wanted to know, *why*? Whoever it was didn't know, just that he had died in the Long Island Railroad station, waiting for a train to take him to New York. What could I do to help? Nothing, the details were being taken care of.

I stared out the window at the silent snow in the city streets. The *deadly* snow, I should have added, but I didn't know that until Mary told me. The *F & SF* office had phoned Cyril and asked him to come to the city. He'd cleared the driveway to get the car out—which Mary bitterly said was *her* job; that was their agreement and he'd stuck to it before that fatal morning—and had driven to the station, parked there and gone to the platform, and there he had died.

It was the last snowfall of the winter.

H. L. Gold

Los Angeles, Cal.